FIRE AND

CHAINS

SHANNON REBER

Published by Magic Fire Publishing

ISBN: 9798721207990

Chapter 1

"The family is the first essential cell of human society."

Pope John XXIII

Fifteen Years Ago

Fire. Pain. Bound. She couldn't move. Jade knew it wasn't real, though that knowledge didn't make it any easier to take. She wanted to run, to free herself from the memory, although her mind held her fast.

She watched as fire ate at the walls and felt the smoke choke her, but she couldn't move. Jade had wriggled and squirmed, the pain in her wrists making it difficult for her to even focus on the fire. She needed to run. Her momma said no, though.

Her mind cried out with a mix of horror and relief when she looked at the woman who stood over her, the knife in her hand gleaming both with Jade's blood and with the flames. "Momma, please," she had moaned, coughing as smoke saturated the air.

She remembered the look in her mom's eyes when she leaned down and laid her finger over Jade's lips. "Hush, love. It will be over soon. The devil will take you and give me a good girl instead. No more wickedness," she had crooned and sat on the edge of the bed, smiling as she stared at the blood that ran down Jade's arms.

No. She could not let her mind show her that horror for even one more moment. She had to break free, so with a monumental effort, she dug her fingernails deep into her palms until the pain made those fiery images fade from her mind.

Jade blinked and shook her head. Birdsong filled the air, mixed with the sounds of summer all around her. A young boy fished in the pond. The sun warmed her skin, and insects buzzed. It all brought her back to the moment. Her body relaxed as she took in the surrounding scene.

There was no fire. It was over. Several years had passed since that horrible night. She was safe. She knew it was true, although sometimes, the skin on the back of her neck crawled like she was being watched.

She shivered. Her fingers moved involuntarily to trace the scars her mom had left on her wrists. Sometimes, she felt as though it was nothing more than a nightmare. Other times, the past felt more real than the life she led.

She cleared her throat and stared out at the pond. Its waters were warm, its banks covered by waving grasses, rocks, and trees. Her step-brother sat on the shore with a fishing pole in his hand, staring out at the bobber that rested on the water's surface.

The house that was visible through the trees looked like it had come from a home and garden ad. Each line drew the eye to the next, each flower and stone in the place where it looked most natural. It was a wide ranch with large windows in every room that looked out onto the beauty of nature all around. A woman sprawled out in a cushy chair on the screened-in porch, pretending to read a book, though really drawing the attention of the man who sat next to her

They were a striking couple, both in their mid-thirties, as near perfect as a couple could appear The man was tall with dark hair, his skin relatively fair, his eyes the color of ferns. The woman was curvy and dark, her skin a rich olive, her eyes the color of chocolate.

Jade watched them, an ache in her chest while a pounding filled her ears. Resentment took the place of the relief she had felt mere moments before. Her scowl turned her youthful face to something old, haggard and nearly ugly.

"Why do you always look like that when you look at my mom?" the boy asked as he peered at her.

Jade blinked, fighting back the anger inside her. "How do I look, Mase?" she asked, trying to make her smile appear natural.

He shrugged. "You look like an old lady me and mom used to live by. She was super grumpy and always yelled at me every time I made a noise in the hallway."

Jade let out an unforced laugh, her posture relaxed. "Mase, I love being compared to nasty old ladies. Thanks tons. Now, you want to see if you can out-run me?" she asked as she stood and stretched like a cat, her chin tipped in challenge.

Mase beamed and nodded as he shouldered his fishing pole, and she took his tackle box.

Jade got into her running stance. "Ready. Set. Go!" she shouted, and they were off.

The path they used was well-trimmed and easy to navigate. Their house was one of only a few that the path led to and each resident worked to keep the area clean and well taken care of.

The warm breeze that blew through the woods should have been comforting, though something felt of to Jade. It sounded wrong, as though the ground itself whispered to her.

You're wicked. The devil's spawn. Wicked girl.

She shook that feeling of as she glanced over, surprised to find that Mase was still right next to her He had gotten faster. Much faster. She was impressed, though she was also a little annoyed. She enjoyed being the fastest runner on her cross-country team at school. The fact a nine-year-old was the same speed as her meant she had a lot of work to do to improve.

Jade ruffled his hair when they reached the gate in the fence at the same time. "You are the man, Mase. Want to see if my dad will grill us some veggie bugers for lunch?" she asked while they walked toward the house to cool down.

Mase whooped and pumped his fist in the air. "I thought it was gunna suck when Mom said you guys are vegans, but your dad makes the best food I ever ate. He's so cool. My dad can't make nothing to eat. When I go to his house, we eat pizza every meal."

"Oh, come on. You like pizza," she said, following the stone path though the garden and up to the house.

They placed Mase's fishing gear in a small shed next to the garage. Jade set the tackle box on a shelf, carefully aligning the edges so they were square. She nodded in an approving way and closed the door, her eyes fixed on Mase as they walked up the steps to the deck.

He shrugged, "Bruce makes good food, so that makes me miss you guys a ton when I'm at my dad's. I keep wondering what you're eating, 'cause it gets boring to eat pizza all the time."

Jade's face wanted so badly to turn down in her habitual scowl at the sight of her dad's wife, but she forced herself to smile. "Hey Dad, me and Mase are starving. Would you grill us some veggie burgers for lunch?"

Bruce looked up from his book and pursed his lips. "Looked to me like Mase worked up more of the appetite than you did," he said, smirking in an obvious way at Mase.

She shrugged, trying not to show her irritation at his reminder of how Mase had almost beaten her "He did, but I could still use some food. What do you say?"

The woman eyed Jade as though she looked at a worm that Mase used for bait. "You know that you're verging on becoming a woman, don't you?"

Jade curled her lip. "I know how old I am," she said, violently rolling her shoulders as though her clothes had become uncomfortable.

Portia leaned forward, showing off her curves. "Most fourteen-year-old girls aren't as high maintenance as you are with your allergies and food choices. You should start dressing more like a woman so guys will pay attention to you," she said, running her hand over her hair

Jade smiled as sharp as a blade. "At least I'm not a total tramp and I'm way less high maintenance than you are, Portia," she spat out and stomped into the house.

She knew she'd have to pay for her disrespect to her step-mom, though right then, she didn't care. She hated the woman with a passion. More, she hated how insecure she felt after those altercations. She trudged into her bedroom and glanced into the mirror, wondering if men would ever admire her the way they admired Portia. She kind of wanted them to sometimes, although the idea of being anything like her step-mom made her want to vomit.

She scowled when her dad stepped into her room and let out the heavy sigh that had become his signature move. He walked over to put his arm around her shoulders. "Why do you do that, Jade?" he asked, looking at her in the mirror.

She stepped away from him and crossed her arms. "Why don't you care when she says things like that to me? Why do you only care if I say something back? She swore at me yesterday and you didn't say a word, but I told her to shut up and I got in trouble. I mean, seriously, it's like since she's got huge boobs and dangles them in your face all the time, you don't even care that she's such a jerk."

Bruce ran his hand over his mouth. "I am talking to you, Jade. You have no idea what Portia and I talk about, so do not tell me what I do and do not say. I want an answer to the question I asked you. Why do you find it necessary to provoke? You get the kind of look on your face like you're ready to gouge her eyes out?"

Tears filled her eyes. "I want Mom to come back. I have wanted her back so bad that I'd cry myself to sleep every night. Now, you married Portia, and she hates me. What if Mom gets better and comes back to us? What if--"

"Jade, that is not going to happen. Your mom can never just recover. It's impossible. She is where she can be as comfortable as possible. You know that," he said, wiping a few of the tears from her cheeks. "I'm asking you to give Portia a break, to give her a chance. If you don't, you're going to ruin one of the best things that has happened to me. I am asking you to put aside your differences and show Portia the girl that I love," he said, leaning down to kiss the top of her head. "Now, you want to help me slice the vegetables?"

She sniffed and nodded, walking with him into the kitchen.

They didn't speak while they prepared lunch, although it was no longer uncomfortable. Father and daughter worked well together, the routine something they both enjoyed. It helped to calm the rest of the tension between them.

Mase jumped up and down when they walked out onto the patio a few minutes later. "Guess what, Jade!" he said, his smile so wide that every one of his teeth showed.

"Umm, you're the first nine-year-old in the world to break the sound barrier while you're running?"

He laughed and shook his head. "Nope. My brother's coming over. Mom says he got me a present, so he's coming over to give it to me."

Jade raised her brows. "Are you sure that's why he's coming?"

Mase nodded and bounced from foot to foot. "Him and his girlfriend are coming in a few hours and they're staying for a few days. Mom says Tanner's girlfriend is super nice. Maybe you and her can be friends!" he said, running into the house before anything more could be said.

Jade looked at her dad, her expression clouded by worry. "Tanner's never bought him a present in his life. The only time he comes over is when he wants money. How's she going to pull this one off?"

Bruce placed the veggies on the grill, basting them with a combination of lemon zest and garlic. "Why don't you go ask, without saying anything insulting in the least."

She set her jaw and squared her shoulders in preparation for the battle.

Jade walked back to the chair where Portia sat, her eyes fixed on the trees. "Mase says Tanner's coming over."

Portia snapped the book closed and pulled a thin shirt around herself. "He and his girlfriend should be here in a few hours."

"I was just wondering what you bought for Mase. He's really excited about the present," she said in a far softer voice

17

than she'd used so far

Portia looked out at the trees as well. "I bought him a drone. I thought he'd have a good time flying it though the trees. I - Jade, you won't tell him I bought it, will you? I want him to think that Tanner thought of him, wanted to give him something."

She smiled. "Your secret's safe with me. Mase is the best brother. I don't want to hurt him at all, ever"

Portia stood up. "You are not his sister."

Jade lifted her chin. "You don't have to be related to somebody for them to be family."

Portia stepped closer, her voice pitched low enough that only Jade could hear her. "Listen to me, you little brat. My son is nothing to you. Whatever kind of freak you really are, I don't care."

"What are you talking about?" Jade breathed, again hearing the voice in her head. *Wicked girl. Creatures like you shouldn't be allowed to live.*

She threw her hands up and jabbed a finger at Jade. "You may have your father fooled, but I see through you. I see what you can do."

A wintry smile passed over Jade's face and she took a small step closer to the woman. "Maybe you should watch your step if you think I'm so dangerous. Wouldn't want something terrible to happen to you," she hissed and raised her hands, flicking her fingers.

Portia flinched, turning away with a sneer. "Freak," she muttered under her breath.

With a victorious smile, Jade turned to leave. She glanced back to look at Portia, the words in her mind coming out before she had thought them through. "I'll never love you and you'll never love me, but I will always love Mase and I will always be a good sister to him," she said and walked away.

Chapter 2

"Mystery creates wonder and wonder is
the basis for man's desire to understand."

Neil Armstrong

Present Day

"Mr. Burke?" a voice asked as Declan picked up his phone, staring dazedly at the clock.

"What?" he asked, running his hand over his eyes, trying to wake up enough to focus.

"You're Declan Burke, the reporter that does investigative stories on channel five, right?" the voice asked, sounding slurred.

"How did you get this number?" Declan asked groggily as he sat up to turn on the light, rubbing his eyes again as the ache filled them.

"Have you ever heard of Mason DaCosta, the fighter?"

"Yeah. Your point?"

"I'm Mase. I got your name and found you because I need your help. I - please. I need your help."

Declan sighed and stood up, moving toward the kitchen. "Okay, how so?" he asked as he flipped on his cofee pot, understanding that he would get no moe sleep that night.

"I don't want to do this on the phone. Can you meet me or something?"

"No, not unless I know what this is about."

Mase sighed into the phone. "They're screwing it up. I know they ae. They're going to kill her, they said they would. I have to find her I have to."

Declan rolled his eyes. "Kid, you'e going to have to be a lot moe specific. Tell me what you want of me."

"I want you to help me find my sister. Last week, she didn't show up at work and I went over to her place to see what was up and it was a mess. Thee was blood on the wall and they left this note. It said they'd kill her if we called the cops and that they'd be calling with their demands. They never called. They never called, and it's been six days."

Declan nodded, looking down at the pad that he had been taking notes on. "Are you high, Mase?" he asked in as patient a voice as he could muster

"I don't use drugs. I'm kind of drunk. I didn't know what to do, so I was - they're going to kill her, man," he said, a panicked sound in his voice.

"Okay Mase, I need for you to listen to me. I want you to hang up with me and get an Uber. I want you to tell them to take you to the Sacred Heart Catholic Church in Raleigh. It's close to Nash Square. I'll help you if I can, but you have to meet me."

"I'll be there," he said without the slightest hesitation.

Declan smiled, feeling alert despite how little sleep he'd gotten over the last few weeks. He jogged into his bedroom and pulled on jeans and a t-shirt. He hurried back into the kitchen, pouring the coffee into two large travel mugs and picking up his bag that contained all he would need to begin the initial interview.

As always, when following a lead that he wasn't certain of, he texted a picture of the notes he'd taken along with the date, time of the call, and the location of the meet to his producer.

He felt good while he hurried out of the building and got into his car His heart pounded, giddy at the prospect of a fresh case. He felt a sharp concern as well, something that made him a good and compassionate reporter.

On the TV screen, he appeared to be an average man with a quiet attractiveness that was appealing. His long, Greek nose and soft brown eyes gave him a look of dignity, though his charming smile was his best feature. He was a tall man, not particularly slim, not particularly broad, merely a man of knowledge and interest, concern and likeability.

As he pulled in down the block from

the church, that smile came to his lips. It was the place where he had received the tip for the first big story of his career. He had, since that day, sent all of those that he wasn't certain of to that place.

He parked his car and walked up the street slowly, keeping his eyes open to all things that could be suspicious. It was a quiet night, one where most of the city seemed to be asleep. That was unusual, making his back twitch as he glanced over his shoulder, once, twice, three times, before he convinced himself that no one had followed him.

He walked to the steps of the church and sat down, taking the first drink of his coffee. He let out a small moan when the caffeine hit his system. He reached into his pocket to take out a pack of cigarettes, lighting one while he watched a car pull up in front of the church. The smoke and the coffee gave him the jump in his system that he needed to focus, to ask the right questions, to be the reporter he needed to be.

His eyes widened as the man stepped out of the Uber Mase appeared to be in his mid-twenties and had a nearly model-like beauty. His hair was dark, cut in a vicious buzz cut, his skin a rich olive that complimented his square, masculine features. The man's eyes came up to meet his, and Declan could see the desolation that looked so out of place on such a man.

Declan nodded as Mase walked up the steps and sat down next to him. "I've seen you fight once or twice. You're good," he said by way of greeting, handing over the cup of coffee.

Mase shrugged, his ears turning red while he tipped his chin down. "I've seen you on the news. You really bring down a drug ring?" he asked, taking a drink of the coffee.

Declan tipped his cup in acknowledgement. "How much have you had to drink tonight, Mase?"

"Few beers, few shots. You want a

drug test before we talk?" He appeared earnest, sincerely asking if that would be necessary.

Declan pursed his lips. "I just need to know how reliable your information will be tonight."

"I'm reliable. I don't really drink though, so maybe you should double check my information." He took a long drink of the coffee, his eyes still turned down.

He chuckled. "If you're alert enough to tell me that, you're good by me." He turned, looking hard at the young man. "How old are you, Mase?"

"Twenty-four."

"How long have you been fighting?"

Mase turned as well, baring his teeth like an angry dog. "This isn't about me. If you came because you wanted to interview me then you can--"

"I'm asking as background. Your age and other information can be found out easily. I'm making conversation so that I can find out what I need to know."

Mase ran his hand over his mouth. "Jade does this stuff for me. She tells me what to say in interviews. I'm not real good with people." He sighed again, taking another drink of coffee. "I've - been fighting professionally for three years. Before that, I fought for reasons. Now, I fight for money. Feels weird." He rubbed the back of his neck.

"Reasons?" Declan asked, surprised by the way he spoke.

He'd expected the kid to be an arrogant blowhard. He hadn't expected such a shy kid, so unlike any boxer that he had ever seen.

Mase scowled. "My first fight was when I found my brother pinning Jade down with his hand up her shirt. I made him pay. That was when I knew I could do this. Tanner is ten years older than me, but I took him down no problem," he said, his eyes damp. "Jade's the best thing that ever happened to me. She's family." A tear slid its way down his cheek, although Mase didn't appear to notice.

Declan jotted down a few observations before he pressed on. "Tell me what happened to her"

Mase's face changed to that of the fighter. He became cold and hard, nearly unrecognizable. "Last week, I had this big interview, one of the biggest of my career. I suck at interviews, so Jade always comes with me, tells me what to say. She gives me a layout of the questions they'll ask and helps me practice. Well, she just wasn't there, and I gave the worst interview. I was pissed and went over to her place after I called everywhere looking for her. It was a wreck. Her stuff was everywhere, shattered and smashed. There was this spot of blood on the wall. Two spots. It was right where her nose would be, like they slammed her head into the wall right there. I think somebody took her, beat the crap out of her from what I could tell. Whoever it was left a note." He swallowed, looking on the vege of tears yet again. "It said, Jade will pay the price of her life if you contact the police. Gather together all that matters to you and be ready to pay the price when we call you. The price will be her life if you do not comply."

Declan raised his brows. "That's kind of flowery. Are you sure it's accurate?" he asked.

He nodded and sniffed again before he ran his hand over his face. "They say it's Jade's writing. They say she's just--" he stopped, looking at Declan with a deep and vicious sorrow. "Her mom's got Huntington's disease. Tried to kill Jade when she was a kid. Bruce, Jade's dad, got there just in time to save them both. Bruce's been Jade's life ever since." He shook his head with fervor "She's scared to death of turning out like her mom, goes to the doctor and to a shrink to make sure she's all good all the time. She's not crazy, and she did not do this. I know it."

Declan made a few more notes. "I assume you went to the cops."

He nodded. "Bruce decided it was a good idea. But the kidnappers haven't called to make any demand at all, so there's nothing for the cops to follow. She's just - gone." He rubbed a hand over his face before he glugged down the last of his coffee.

"How are you with money? If they call and make monetary demands, are you financially capable of meeting them?"

He cleared his throat. "I'm not loaded, but I'll do anything and everything I can. I have to find her I need to know she's okay. She's all I have."

Declan took a long drag on his cigarette. "I'm going to need more information, Mase," he said, then nodded and rose. "Let's go get some breakfast and you can tell me the rest of it."

Chapter 3

"There is nothing more stimulating than a
case where everything goes against you."

Sir Arthur Conan Doyle

The Present

A short time later, Declan pulled up in
front of a small twenty-four-hour diner. It
was a place he'd been to before, one that
he didn't particularly dislike, nor did he
particularly like it. It worked for his
purpose, so that was all he required.

He peered at Mase, not entirely
certain what to make of the kid. "You
ready for this?" he asked, seeing just how
tired he was.

Mase nodded. "If you can help me
find her, I'll give you the story exclusively,"
he said, dangling that catch phrase as
though it was a carrot and Declan was a
hungry bunny.

"You'll have to sign that for me."

"I will. Just please find her"

"I'll do everything I can," he said,
getting out of the car and moving up to the
diner while his mind mapped out the

story.

A haggard server walked over after they'd sat at a table, smiling at them both. "What can I bring for you?" she asked, twiddling her pen while she waited for their orders.

"Coffee and oatmeal, please," Mase responded, his eyes fixed on the table in front of him.

She frowned at him. "You okay?" she asked, her brow lowered while she gave him a probing gaze.

He nodded, his eyes still down.

Declan smiled, hoping to blow of the tension. "I'll have the same, but we're going to need some waters as well."

She moved off, turning her head to look at the two.

Declan raised his brows. "So you want to tell me the rest of it?" he asked, setting his phone on the table to record their conversation while he sat back.

Mase shook his head. "I told you all I know." His left eye twitched, though that was the only sign he gave he wasn't telling the full truth.

"No, you didn't. You've got a lot of weight on your shoulders. Tell me why you think this is your fault."

He swallowed, resting his hand on the table while he flexed his knuckles wearily. "I was supposed to throw a fight, but I didn't. Jade got me this fight in Vegas, but they offered me a load of money to lose. Jade said no way. She said never throw a fight, so I didn't. A week later she was gone."

"Did you tell the cops this?"

He nodded. "They don't think it has anything to do with anything. I don't get those people. It's so obvious, but they're ignoring it."

Declan let out a slow sigh. "The cops know their jobs, Mase. I'll look and see what they'll tell me. I have some friends in the police department here. It did happen in Raleigh, didn't it?"

Mase nodded.

"I'll see what I can find then," he said, smiling in thanks as the server filled their cups with fresh coffee and set water glasses down in front of both of them.

Mase gulped down his entire glass of water before he dumped several creamers into his coffee. He stirred it methodically, his eyes fixed on that task.

Declan drank his black, the first drink finally making him feel he was ready to face this story. "Tell me about Jade. What does she do, how does she spend her time, how old is she, et cetera?" He pushed his glass of water over hoping it would help to assuage any hangover the kid might have.

Mase stared into his coffee. "She's a publicist. Does most of her work for people around here, like me, but she does some work everywhere. She's good. If it wasn't for her, most of us would still be poor" He shrugged. "She's twenty-nine and does healthy things. She's a big runner, does triathlons. She trains for them all the time. Me and her run together a couple times a week and she's good. I don't have to slow up for her at all. For hobbies, I don't really know. She's dating this guy that's a big sports fan, so they go to a lot of games. It doesn't matter what sport, he likes it and she goes along,"

"His name?"

"Ronnie Maurer. I don't like him. He's not serious about her I think she knows it."

Declan bit back his surprise. He knew Ronnie, although he didn't suppose it mattered much. He found it surprising that Ronnie hadn't come to him instead of Mase. "Tell me about the day before she disappeared. What did you do that day?" he asked, aware it would be easier to get the details he needed by easing around the subject rather than plowing into it head first.

Mase lifted a single shoulder "The usual. I went for a run at five in the morning, got back at six, got ready, and

37

went to the gym. Trained and sparred until seven that night. I went home, cleaned up, and went on a date. I talked to Jade a couple times, running over the things I was supposed to do, what to wear to the interview, all that. As far as I know, her and Ronnie were going out that night. She likes routine. They only go out on certain days, at certain times, that kind of thing."

Declan jotted that down, finding it to be the most interesting thing he'd heard about the woman so far "Had she said anything to you about something worrying her, anyone following her, odd texts, or threats on social media?"

Mase shook his head. "Nothing," he said, sitting back as the server set the bowls of oatmeal in front of them.

"Can I bring you anything else?" she asked, not looking interested in their answer.

Mase and Declan shook their heads, both lost in thought.

As she walked back into the kitchen, Declan saw Mase glowering out the window of the diner He moved with surprising speed to the door and threw it open. Before Declan could do more than blink, Mase grabbed a man's collar and hauled him into the diner

"What are you doing here?" Mase demanded, shaking the man as he did.

The guy shoved ineffectually at Mase. "Following you. It was the only way to find out what was up," he growled.

Mase shook him all the harder. "If I wanted you to know, I would have told you."

He bared his perfect teeth, looking ready to fight, despite the fact he was nearly half Mase's breadth in muscle. His honey blond hair was well cut, showing off big brown eyes that were shadowed by worry.

Declan stood and moved to where the two faced off. "Ronnie, how's your brother?" he asked in greeting.

He ran his hand back through his hair. "Decs, what are you doing here with him?" he jabbed a finger at Mase as though it was an accusation.

Declan suppressed his chuckle with difficulty. "Looks like we're all trying to do the same thing. Why don't you come and sit down? You can answer the questions I was going to ask you later on today." Declan moved back to the table without waiting for a response.

Mase and Ronnie glared at each other, but both followed him to the table.

Mase turned his angry gaze on Declan when he slid back into his seat. "Why didn't you say that you knew him?"

Declan raised his brows. "For the same reasons you haven't told me everything."

Ronnie slumped into a chair at the end of the booth they sat in. "Decs and my brother were in law school together" He looked at Declan. "So you're going to help look for Jade?"

Declan added the raisins and brown sugar the server had provided to his oatmeal, his eyes fixed on that task. "I am. You want to fill me in?" he asked in a measured tone.

Ronnie ran his hands over his face. "Jade's weird. She's so absolutely determined that everything has to be normal that it makes life abnormal. We've been dating for a couple of months and it's been okay. She'd be cool if she could let go of whatever's holding her back. Anyway, we went on our usual date, then the next day, she was just gone."

"Did she say anything to you about being afraid, anyone following her, anything?"

"Nothing. She's not the type to share things like that." He ran his hand over his face again. "The only information we've got is that note, and they say she wrote it. They showed me the proof, but I just didn't see it. The thing is, it's just not like her to even try to get attention. She never wants attention. I hate to say this, but I'm with Mase. I just want to know why these people haven't called to ask the ransom. They said they would, but they haven't. It doesn't make sense."

Declan didn't respond to that. Instead, he took out his tablet and handed it to Mase. "Write down every piece of pertinent information. Every piece," he said and started his oatmeal, watching the two as they argued and debated what was pertinent and what was not. He sighed inwardly, having a horrible feeling that the news they would receive would most definitely be bad.

Chapter 4

"Whoever is careless with the truth in small matters cannot be trusted with important matters."

Albert Einstein

Fifteen Years Ago

"Jade Amora Rosenberg, get in here. Now," Bruce's voice called through the house.

Jade looked up from the book she'd been reading, startled by the tone. She stood up, walking into the living room, startled all the more when she saw the look on Bruce's face. "What's wrong?" she asked, her heart beating at an irregular rhythm.

Bruce pointed to the couch as though he was too angry to even speak.

Jade sat down, her hands twitching nervously, feeling a horrible desire to run from the man she had loved and trusted all of her life.

Bruce took one long breath, then walked over to sit on the coffee table in front of her. "Do you have something you want to tell me?" he demanded while his eyes probed hers.

She thought hard, unsure what she could have done to bring on such a reaction. "I - I don't - I don't think so," she stammered, and the pillow next to her fell over.

He held out his hand to show her an empty condom wrapper "Do you want to explain what this was doing in your room?"

She stared at the wrapper, then at him, shaking her head. "No, Dad. I've never done that. I promise, I swear. I really didn't."

He looked hard at her, like he meant to pull the truth from her. "Why would you lie to me, Jade? If you're going to be that kind of girl, I'd rather know about it than have you lie to me." He frowned. "You're grounded. I don't know how long. Just get out of my sight," he said, standing to leave the room.

She ran after him. "Dad, no. I really haven't. I really, really haven't. I've never even kissed a guy. I swear"

He didn't turn, didn't look at her, merely walked out of the house.

Jade burst into tears. She ran to her room and threw herself down on her bed. She wept at the fact that her dad had not believed her when she'd spoken the absolute truth. She had never in her life kissed a boy, let alone sleep with one in her father's house.

Her tears racked her body while a roaring filled her ears. She knew who was to blame, and she swore that she would have her revenge.

"Jade?" a voice said from her side.

She rolled to her other side.

Mase walked around her bed and sat down, his posture stooped. "I'm sorry, Jade. Tanner's mad at you, so he brought his girlfriend in here. He told Mom that he heard you, so she came to look and see if she could find proof. I'm real sorry. Want me to go tell Bruce?"

She sniffed, wiping tears from her face with a shaky hand. "No. I don't want you to tell Dad. If he can't believe me, I don't care. I'm not going to go and try to prove it to him. I shouldn't have to," she said, her face morphing into that angry, resentful expression that made her look so different.

Mase's lip quivered. "Tanner's a jerk. I don't like him. I thought he was so cool, but I think he's a big jerk now. I'm going to crash the drone he gave me into a tree," he said, his breaths loud while his eyes bulged.

Jade sat up and dried her face. "Don't do that, Mase. Tanner didn't buy you the drone. Your mom bought it for you. She didn't want you to know what a jerk Tanner is."

He opened his mouth, the tears in his eyes drying instantly. "Mom lied to me?"

"Listen to me, Mase. Your mom did a nice thing in buying you that present. It was a good thing to do. Your mom loves you a ton. Remember that. Sometimes it's good to tell lies when it helps somebody we love feel better. Do you hear me?"

He stood up, his face relaxed as he picked up her book, handed it back to her and walked from her room.

Jade sniffed, staring at her book. After a moment, she hurled it across the room, her teeth gritted so tight it made her ears ring.

"Is there anything you want to tell me?" Bruce asked from the door, his arms folded, his brows raised.

Jade froze, a fawn in the crosshairs. Black spots filled her vision while dizziness washed over her

He walked into the room and sat down on the bed with a deep sigh. "I'm sorry. I should have believed you. I should have asked more questions."

"Why didn't you? Why did you just believe the worst?" she whispered.

He turned his head to look at her "I was scared, Jade. Your mom, before I knew she was sick, she started lying to me. It was about little things at first, then about everything. It got to a point where I never believed anything she said unless I could verify it." He swallowed, leaning his elbows on his knees. "You get a look on your face sometimes, generally when you're mad about something, you remind me of her."

Jade's eyes filled with tears. She walked over to pick up the book she had thrown. Her tears dripped onto the floor while she clutched the book to her chest. "How could you think that I'd be like her? I would never - never I'm not like her."

Bruce walked over and pulled her to her feet, wrapping his arms around her. "You're right, Jade. You're nothing like her at all. That was my fear, my wrong, not yours. You are nothing like her."

She clung to him, her body shaking with sobs. The fire crackled around her, her mom's voice filling the room. *Wicked girl. Satan's mark is on your soul.*

Those images flashed through her

mind like a horror movie of terror and pain. She knew intellectually that her mom was sick, that her disorder had caused her to lash out. But she also knew there was something different about her. She could sense it and she knew her dad sensed it as well.

Bruce pulled her back after a moment, looking hard into her eyes. "Jade, wake up," his voice said.

She blinked, opening her eyes to find that her dad stood over her, his teeth clenched so tight that the muscle in his jaw bulged. Tears filled her eyes again. She had merely dreamed of her father's apology, dreamed that he loved and believed her.

"Sit up," he said in an icy voice.

Jade sat up, trying to suppress the tears that swam in her eyes.

Bruce sat down on the bed and set a small, thin, pink box between them. "I hate this, Jade, but if you're going to be that kind of girl, you will not take chances with pregnancy. Huntington's is genetic. You don't want to take a chance on passing that to your child. I'd hoped to have this conversation with you when you were older, but it looks like it needs to happen now."

Jade gaped at the box, then at her father, her palms tingling. "When have you ever seen me with a guy?" she asked through her teeth and her book fell of the bed, hitting the floor with a thunk.

"That is not--"

"Screw you, Dad. I told you the truth, and it is still the truth. If my mom lied to you or not. I've never slept with anybody and I am not taking those pills. Shove them up your butt." She stood and stomped from the room, a vibration filling her, as though there was a live wire inside her.

She made it two steps before Bruce's hand wrapped like a vice around her arm. He hauled her back into her room, his face nearly demented by anger

51

"What makes you think you can speak to me in that way?" he growled in a low voice.

"I wouldn't have about half an hour ago, but now that you think I'm a slut, what does it matter? Why don't I just start being the person you think I am?"

"Jade--"

"No, I'm a slut. I bring guys here and screw their brains out in my bedroom. I'm easy. I'm surprised that you only found one condom wrapper Get out of my room, Bruce. I have some dirty, nasty things to do," she spat, turning her back on him as the vibration inside her increased and the things on her dresser shifted around as though of their own accord.

"Jade--"

"No. I'm not listening to you. I don't care what my mom did. I don't care. I don't want to talk to you. I don't want to--" she could no longer keep her voice steady. It broke, her body curling into a small defensive ball.

Bruce stared at her, his mouth working silently for a few moments. He took a step toward the door, then stopped, appearing lost for words.

"She didn't do anything!" Mase shouted, rushing into the room. "Tanner got mad at her when him and his girlfriend came over last weekend and he came back. He did it, then told Mom that he heard Jade doing it, so Mom told you 'cause she wants you to think Jade's bad. Tanner--"

"Shut up, Mase. I told you to shut up," Jade wailed, her tear-stained face coming up from the pillow.

Bruce looked down at Mase, folding his arms over his chest. "How do you know this?" he asked, a muscle twitching in his cheek.

Mase folded his arms as well, looking up with all the defiance he could muster. "I heard him laughing about it. He played you, Bruce."

53

Bruce turned his head to look at his daughter. "Looks like you and I need to talk."

She sniffled. "I talked. I don't have anything else to say."

"Then you can listen." He held out his hand to her. "Take a walk with me, Jade."

Jade sniffed, aware that she couldn't refuse. She would have to pay for all the things she had said. She wiped tears from her face, a sour taste in her mouth while her pulse throbbed in her neck.

Dinner was a quiet affair that evening. None of them could hold a conversation, the only sounds in the room the scrape of fork on plate. It was an uncomfortable meal, though gradually, the tension eased as they ate.

Mase looked up from his plate and smiled at Bruce. "You cook good. I like this," he said as he swallowed his last bite.

Bruce smiled slightly. "I'm glad you

54

like it, Mase. You can call me Betty Crocker."

He grinned. "Okay, Betty. Can we have dessert?"

Portia huffed. "I'd say you've eaten enough today, Mason. With the way you eat, you're going to turn into a fatty."

He squished his eyebrows together, lifting his shirt to show his skinny form. "I'm the smallest guy in my class, but I eat more than most of them do. Can't I just have one more scoop of the bean and avocado stuff? I don't have to have dessert."

Portia shook her head. "I'm tired of watching you eat."

"Close your eyes," Jade suggested, scooping more into Mase's bowl with a sweet smile as she took a bite of her own.

Portia's nostrils flared, but she didn't speak, her teeth bared like she fought to hold back her furious diatribe.

Bruce leaned back in his chair "Will you two do the dishes for me? I need a couple of hours to finish that model I've been working on, then I thought maybe we could play chess."

Mase beamed. "Awesome! I'm totally going to kick your butt this time."

Bruce laughed. "Maybe. You did come pretty close last time." He turned to smile at his wife. "Come on, Portia. Let's leave them to this," he said and moved around the table, resting his hand on Jade's shoulder when he passed.

As they walked from the house, Jade smirked at Mase. "Last time we were at the store, I bought some cookies for you. They're in the cupboard. You can have a couple while we're cleaning this mess up," she said, walking into the kitchen to grab the package.

Mase ran into the kitchen eagerly, though shot Jade a worried look. "But Mom doesn't want me to get fat and stuff."

"If you keep exercising, you won't get fat. I don't think it matters, though. A lot of very nice, very pretty people have a little bit of fat, so it's just something you're going to have to make up your mind about. Are you going to be the kind of person that will turn up your nose when you see somebody that's overweight, or will you look at the person's heart, the way they act?"

Mase considered this, looking at the cookie package, then he looked up at Jade. "I'd still think you were pretty if you were fat. Even when you're mad and your face gets mean, I still think you're pretty. Does that count?"

Jade chuckled, kissing the top of his head. "That's very nice of you, Mase. But see, I know that I'll never be pretty. I'm just not the kind of girl to be pretty, or to have boyfriends and stuf. I'm just going to live the rest of my life making sure you're okay, making sure you get a cookie when you feel like it."

He devoured his treat, his eyes fixed on her pensively. "Jade - are you magic?" he asked in a near whisper

Jade's heart picked up its pace. "Magic? What do you mean, Mase?" she asked, the voice in her head jeering,*You're wicked. Evil. You're the devil's girl*

Mase chewed a second cookie far slower. "When you get mad, stuf moves. Like all by itself. Are you magic?" he asked again.

She let out a shaky laugh. "Ther's no such thing as magic, Mase," she said and rushed back into the dining oom to gather up their plates.

Mase followed her, still giving her that same contemplative look. "It don't matter if you're magic or if you're fat. The guys on the bus all think you'e super hot. They all talk about you."

Jade frowned. "All those guys see is physical features. They don't know me and they don't want to. Do you see what I mean?" she asked, loading the rinsed plates into the dishwasher

He nodded. "I see. But Jade, you have a pretty heart too. You always take care of me and stuff. I think you're super cool and I don't really care what you look like."

"Thank you, Mase. I think you're super cool too, and I am going to spend the rest of my life being the best sister you ever had."

Chapter 5

"Memory is a complicated thing, a relative
to truth, but not its twin."

Barbara Kingsolver

The Present

Declan looked at the tablet he'd asked Mase to write the pertinent information of the case on and sighed. Everything he'd noted made it appear he wanted to take the blame, to punish himself for whatever had happened to Jade. Ronnie's thoughts on the matter were identical, his desire to blame Mase screaming from the tablet.

Declan took his phone from his pocket and played that first interview over again. As he listened, he took more detailed notes, typing out things he thought would help him find the truth. He sat back when he had finished, thinking that for the first time in his life, he may have found a story that he could not tell.

The twists and turns, along with the utter lack of information, might make for a very interesting story, but he wasn't certain it could be told in a news segment.

He looked the notes over, wondering if he had come upon the story for his first book.

He checked the time on his phone, seeing that it was just past nine. He nodded and rose, gathering his laptop and tablet along with the list of people to contact. He smiled just slightly as he walked yet again from his condo. His smile froze when he saw Ronnie just getting out of his car.

"Decs, I need to talk to you." There were dark circles under his eyes, though his chin was high.

"About?"

Ronnie shrugged. "I want to help. I have to help."

Declan raised his brows, though hit the record app on his phone. "Why do you need to help?" he asked.

Ronnie peered over Declan's shoulder. "I wasn't good to her I wasn't good for her. The night before she disappeared - I broke it off with her. I was getting sick of it all, so I just told her we were through."

"Why didn't you mention it this morning?"

Ronnie let out a derisive snort. "I assume you saw Mase. He's always looking for some reason to point a finger at me, tell me what I do wrong. I'm sick of listening to the guy. If I'd told him I broke it off with her, he'd have gone ballistic and probably thrown me out. I do care about her, I just don't want to date somebody that's so - troubled."

Declan let out a slow breath. "What do you mean, troubled?"

"I don't even really mean that. It's just that she's gorgeous, perfect, but she's torn up. I just wanted somebody cool and fun. I mean, she was good in bed. Outstanding, really, but she's just more complicated than I like," he said lamely.

Declan lit a cigarette, taking in a long drag before he spoke. "So if you're not into the complicated woman, why is it so important to you to help find her?"

Ronnie cleared his throat. "She, uh, she's - pregnant."

"Yours?" Declan asked, a ball of worry filling his stomach.

He nodded.

"So now that she's gone, you're concerned for your kid that she's carrying?" Declan asked, doing his best to keep his voice as unemotional as possible.

"Gone? Don't you think there's any way she can be alive?"

"I would be surprised if she was alive. Something rings true in Mase's description of the place. I believe they kidnapped her to be held for ransom, but something went wrong. They haven't called either because she's dead, or they are. In either case, there's little to no hope of finding her," he said, watching closely to see what Ronnie would let slip next.

"Decs, let me help you find out what happened."

Declan shook his head. "Go home, Ronnie. Call your brother and tell him all of it, have him advise you. I can't and I won't advise you," he said in a chilly voice, walking past the younger man to get into his car.

He watched Ronnie drive away, wondering just how wrong he could be about a person. He never would have guessed that Ronnie Mauer would tell him such a story, but he could see clearly that it was the absolute truth. Ronnie had dumped his girlfriend when she had gotten pregnant. He shook his head, wanting more than anything to tell this tale to Mase just to watch him tear Ronnie limb from limb.

He drove as quickly as he could to get to the police station. He played back the conversation he had just had with Ronnie, wondering what other secrets would be revealed as he delved further into the story.

He walked into the police station and looked around with a small smile. He lifted his hand in greeting to several old friends before he got to the front desk where a middle-aged officer sat.

"May I help you?" she asked, smiling at him in the way he had gotten used to over the last few years, as though she wanted to ask him for an autograph or to take a selfie with her

He gave her a polite smile, neither encouraging nor discouraging her recognition. "Is Detective Talib in?" he asked.

The phone next to her rang, so she simply handed him a visitor's badge and pointed back toward a desk.

Declan pinned the badge to his shirt and walked through the office space, then stopped at a desk that was so cluttered by papers and trash, it was a wonder the man who sat in front of it could even figure out what he was doing.

"Never learned that organization thing, I see," Declan said, grinning as his old partner looked up.

Frank leaned back in his chair

folding his skinny arms over his ample belly. "Decs, you look fat on TV," he said with a small smile.

Declan patted his flat stomach. "The camera does add ten pounds. My mom thinks I look just wonderful on the screen and my dad rolls his eyes, telling everybody about his crazy son."

Frank snorted out a laugh, standing to clap Declan on the shoulder "You are one crazy guy. What is this, your third career? Lawyer, cop, and reporter. The middle career's the only one that makes any sense."

"That's what my dad thinks too. You and he should get together You can criticize my career all you want."

He motioned for Declan to sit in a chair covered by papers. "Let's just talk about you setting me up with that weather girl."

Declan grinned, scooping the papers up, and setting them on his lap as he sat. "Not a chance, Frankie. I know you too well."

He rolled his eyes and made a hurry up gesture with his hand. "So what are you looking into, Decs?"

"The disappearance of Jade Rosenberg. You heading up the investigation?"

Frank sighed and rubbed at his eyes. "No, I'm not. There's nothing to investigate. The note was in her handwriting. She's messing with them. That's all."

Declan knew he couldn't record his conversation with Frank, so he focused his attention as fully as possible on everything Frank said, every inflection and expression. "I wouldn't be here if I agreed with you on that. Something stinks about the whole situation."

Frank's eyes tightened. "That's the reporter, not the cop talking. There's nothing to report, Decs. That woman's dicking with them and will either show up next week with a tan and a story about a horrible abduction where she miraculously escaped, or she'll never show up just to pay them all back."

Declan narrowed his eyes. "What do you mean, pay them back?"

He scoffed. "Looks like you haven't been given too many of the details," he said in a superior tone, lifting a finger to tick off each point. "In the space of a week, the woman goes to the doctor and finds out she's pregnant. Then she finds out that her mom, who she had always been told was in a nursing home, had been given some kind of experimental drug and was released years before. The mom is now living a relatively quiet life with a husband. Then Jade gets in a bad argument with her dad where he tells her it's altogether possible she's not even his daughter. After that, she has a car accident and gets dumped by her boyfriend. I'd say if anyone had the right to take a swing at her family by disappearing for a while, it's her"

Declan let out a sigh. "I didn't know the entire story. The brother--"

"She has no brother. Mase DaCosta was her step-brother for four years before the parents got divorced."

"Okay, Mase only told me about the kidnapping. Can I see the ransom note?"

Frank shrugged, pulling open a drawer in his desk to take out a folder

Declan raised his brows when he saw the note. It was so neat that it appeared typewritten in a perfect, feminine handwriting. Each letter was perfect and utterly like the others. "A handwritten note is pretty unusual these days," he commented, the back of his neck itching like it always did when the puzzle pieces didn't match the picture.

Frank shrugged again, though didn't comment.

"I can see what you mean about the handwriting." He looked hard at the note, then at the sample of Jade's handwriting. "I've never seen writing like it. It's utterly perfect. Mimicking it would be practically impossible."

Frank tapped his fingers on his desk. "We had experts looking it over and only one of them thought it was a fogery."

Declan shifted the junk on his lap to the floor. "Can I look at the rest?"

He pushed the folder over and leaned back in his chair, watching as his old partner went through the normal routines, the ones that had helped them solve many cases that had seemed insurmountable at the time.

Declan took out the pictures of Jade's condo, his brows furrowed at the state of the place. "My guess is that the woman has some kind of obsessive tendencies to judge by her writing. Something like this would have driven her nuts if she had to look at it for very long." He took out the rest of the pictures, stopping as he got to a picture of the living room. "There's blood there, on the floor." He pointed to a place that was nearly

71

obscured by a broken coffee table.

Frank took the photo, raising his brows. "I saw that as well. What do you make of it?"

Pictures formed a movie in his mind. "I'd guess she put up quite a fight. She's probably badly injured. There's more blood there." He pointed to another dark spot that was nearly obscured by a broken desk. "I'd guess she isn't pregnant anymore after taking that kind of beating. Did Mase say anything about self-defense classes or anything like that, for her to know how to hurt the attacker?"

Frank shook his head. "I didn't ask. With a fighter around, though, you'd have to guess that she would pick things up."

Declan stared at the pictures. "So we'll say she knows how to protect herself, puts up a fight, probably injures him as well. There's no way she's not injured. There's too much damage." He stopped, looking the pictures over again, then looked up at his friend. "Will you let me see it? I really think you might have a murder case here, man. You need to look at this again."

Frank reached behind him to take his suit jacket from the back of his chair and stood up. "Let's look at this thing," he said with a nod.

Chapter 6

"One must seek the truth within -- not without."

Agatha Christie

The Present

"You ever think about coming back?"
Frank asked while he and Declan dove
through the city.

"No, never," Declan replied,
watching as the city went fom businesses
to homes, a metamorphosis he always
enjoyed observing.

"I don't get you, Decs. You were a
good attorney, then you were a great cop,
now you're a reporter. Why do you keep
changing careers?"

He scratched his chin. "I'm in the
same line I've always been in. I'm just
looking for the truth in diferent ways.
Now shut up and let me focus."

Frank smirked and zipped his lips
like a child.

Declan ignored that, simply focusing
on the truths he'd found so far "I'd say
that if there was more than one assailant,

she wouldn't have been able to fight so much, so I'm going to guess that there was just one. How tall is she, body structure, that kind of thing?"

They pulled up in front of a townhouse that looked as though it had come straight from Chicago. The row of buildings were all well cared for and affluent. Each one had some sort of decoration in front, a distinctive feature to set it apart from the place next to it.

"She's a little above average in height, model kind of structure but fit, toned, not just skin and bones like most of them. I have no idea of weight, but I'd be shocked if she was over a hundred-fifteen."

Declan nodded. "So one guy either comes to the door, or is already there when she gets home." He got out of the car and moved up to the door He looked at the steps, and all the windows all around them. "Lots of neighbors. Anybody see anything?"

"Nothing. No one heard or saw anything, but the neighbors on either side were out of town on the days in question."

"Days?"

"Fifteen hours. She's unaccounted for from nine o'clock on Tuesday night, to noon on Wednesday."

Declan rubbed his chin. "If no one saw anything, we can assume this happened in the dead of night," he said and closed his eyes. He allowed Frank to open the door, wanting to get the full impact as he always did.

Pictures formed in his mind, the heat of excitement moving over him. "Dead of the night, a knock sounds on the door and she's frustrated, mad because her boyfriend just dumped her and she's confused. Huntington's is genetic fom what I've read, so she'd fear passing it on. She doesn't know what to do about the baby, or any of it. She comes to the door thinking it's Ronnie wanting to talk, but it's not. It's someone else. So does she let him in, or does he force his way in?" he asked, looking only at the entranceway.

Inside the door was a hand carved table with broken knickknacks on the surrounding floor. The space was minimally decorated, though everything appeared to have a specific space. The fact those few items were broken and scattered on the floor was the biggest red flag he'd seen so far.

"I wouldn't say there was an argument. I'd say he shoved her back, belted her one, and she hit the table. She would have been hurting, but adrenalin would have kicked in, along with training, probably from Mase. I'd say she didn't run because it looks like most of the damage is in a concentrated area." He pointed from the entranceway to a living room.

He walked through the area, nodding as he took in more of the mess. There were slashes in the furnishings and dents in the walls. He could not understand how Frank had gotten the impression that Jade did it as a slap to her family

He gestured to a blanket that was nearly cut in half. "He pulled the knife when he couldn't subdue her immediately, swinging it wildly, mostly to scare her. I'd say it didn't scare her, but focused her. It made her an even more tough opponent." He nodded, seeing an empty space on the marble mantle where something had sat, then the glass toward the center of the room. "She chucked something at him and hit him, which just pissed him of." He examined the reddish brown splotches on the floor. "Have you even typed the blood yet?"

"No."

"Why?" Declan demanded, incredulous.

Frank blew out a breath. "Because we were told not to. The commissioner himself told me this was a scam, and that I had more important cases to work on."

Declan cursed volubly. "Fine. I'll call

in my last favor and get it done myself," he gnarled, jotting himself a note to look into the commissioner when he had a moment.

Frank said something, but Declan wasn't listening.

He looked around the room again, that time seeing small speckles of blood on the floor. "She was cut, but nothing major I'd guess that after he was hit was when he got really vicious. It looks like the next hit would have been the one that brought down the coffee table." He looked at the broken glass around the table, a larger piece that looked to have a small bit of blood remaining on it. "She wouldn't have been moving as quickly as she should after that blow, so he would have gotten her shortly after." He stood straight, walking to the dent in the wall where the blood so clearly stood out. "Her nose is broken, and I'd guess she's concussed. I don't know, man. It looks to me like he killed her. She didn't die here, but I think she's dead."

"What makes you think that?" Frank asked in a contrite tone.

"She hurt him. The average kidnapper won't take kindly to that. She wouldn't have been capable of writing the note when he had finished with her so I'm going to say it's forged. You're looking for a good hand, a steady hand, one that probably hasn't been busted before. Your forger is the key." He turned around the room, looking for anything he might have missed on his first circuit of the space.

Good furniture. Clean lines. Windows that looked out onto a grove of trees behind the townhouses. A bookshelf loaded down with books.

He furrowed his brows as he walked to the bookshelf, seeing that the books had been disarranged slightly. "You guys already dust for prints?"

Frank nodded.

Declan reached behind him, holding out his hand, waiting as Frank placed a pair of rubber gloves into his hand.

He slowly took down one book, then the next, and the next to reveal the space behind them. "That's odd," he said when he saw a small box hidden there.

Frank walked over, his eyes going wide. "And here I thought you'd pull out a recording device that would spill out its secrets for all of us to hear"

Declan reached out reverently and set the box in his hand, opening it with the other. What he saw was a silver cross necklace with a diamond at the center "I figured I'd find a gun. Thought that she would go for the gun and that was why he--" he stopped when he picked up the necklace and saw that its back was blackened as though it had been though a fire.

His heart pounded. He had found his story, had found the beginning to the truth. He had found Jade, not her location, but the woman herself. Her deepest fear lay inside that small box, alongside a necklace that she seemed to have both loved and hated.

Chapter 7

"Silence is a lie that screams at the light."

Shannon L. Alder

Fourteen Years Ago

Jade held out her hand with a grin as they pulled into the parking lot of the mall. "You do know we're both going to need school clothes, right?"

Bruce chuckled as he pulled into a parking place. "That's why I'm coming with you. Look at it this way, Jade. If I come, so do the credit cards," he said as she opened her mouth to protest.

She sighed gustily as she turned to look at Mase, rolling her eyes. "And here I was, thinking you and I were going to the mall so that I could get my bellybutton pierced."

He chuckled. "Think I could get a tattoo?" he asked as they got out of the car.

Bruce ruffled the boy's hair. "That'll be the day."

As they walked into the mall, Mase placed his hand into Bruce's, his breaths quick while he eyed the exits.

An ache filled Jade's throat. She knew Mase preferred to be at home, enough that he mostly remained there instead of even going to a friend's house. She hoped she might help him in some small way, her heart aching at the obvious fear on his face.

"Hey Mase," she said with a smile, "You want to see if we can talk Dad into a tropical ice before we do this school shopping thing?" she asked with a smile that was a bit too bright.

His eyes flicked up to meet hers, a small smile coming to his lips. "That would be awesome. Can we, Bruce?" he asked in a voice so low, it could hardly be heard.

He nodded, handing Jade some cash.

She moved up through the food court to the only place in the mall she could eat from. They made slushies that were nothing more than shaved ice mixed with fruit. It was one of Jade's favorite things. She'd been pleased to find that Mase liked it as much as she did.

Her gaze grew watery when she looked back at Bruce and Mase. She saw that Mase's head was still turned down, as though he was too afraid to look around.

"Watch it," an angry voice said as she bumped into someone.

Her eyes turned back to where she walked, then up to meet the eyes of the boy she had bumped. "Sorry," she said and stepped around him to place her order. "Three strawberry-pineapple ices, please," she said, watching the woman fill the order.

She thought about how cool it was, the way the ice and fruit were mixed in even patterns through the plastic cups. Patterns interested her. Maps. Art. Life itself. It was all varying patterns she could easily get lost in.

Everything other than her She'd never fit. She couldn't explain the strange things that happened around her or why she so often felt as though someone unseen watched her Even there, in the middle of that crowded mall, the back of her neck prickled like there were eyes boring into her.

She turned when she had paid to find the boy she had bumped into standing behind her "I know you," he said with a grin.

She gave him a disdainful look. "I doubt that," she said and stepped around him again.

The boy chuckled, falling into step next to her "You go to my school. What's your name?" he asked, a pleasant and friendly smile on his face.

"If you know me, why don't you know my name?" she asked, not bothering even to look at him.

He snapped his fingers. "It's a color I remember that. It's not Scarlett, but it's kind of close, isn't it?"

She sighed, unsure if it had been him who watched her or if it was someone else. "It's Jade," she told him, feeling as nervous as Mase looked.

"That's it. It suits your green eyes. I'm Todd," he said, smiling even more widely than he did before. "You come with some girls?" he asked with a gesture at her fruit slushies.

"No, I came with my dad and brother."

Todd laughed. "That's got to suck. Want to ditch them and hang with us? We're going to the movies in a little bit."

Jade looked up at him. "I'm no one you want to know. If you knew me, you'd run in the other direction. Just take my word for it," she said, walking to where Bruce and Mase sat.

Bruce raised his brows. "Who was the kid?"

"I don't know. A guy from school." She took a cup out of the carrier and

89

handed one to each of them. "Mase, her's to a wonderful day of Dad spending money on us," she said with a grin as she tapped her cup to his.

Mase shrank closer to her "Thanks, Bruce, and thanks for getting them, Jade," he said in a near whisper

"Absolutely," Jade answered, grinning as she dug her spoon into the sweet treat. "Not bad, is it?"

He shook his head, his eyes fixed on the floor.

When they finished, Jade looked at her hands, wiggling her sticky fingers in front of Mase. "We should probably go wash our hands so we don't get kicked out of our favorite stores for getting strawberry on their clothes."

Mase nodded, his eyes still turned down while he followed Bruce to the bathroom.

Jade laid her hand on Bruce's arm, pulling him to a stop in the bathroom corridor. "Is he okay?" she asked in a whisper.

Bruce nodded. "He's scared of crowds. Nothing to worry about. He's handling it the best way he knows how," he said with a smile as he shooed her into the bathroom.

Later that evening, Jade stood next to her bed carefully folding her new clothes. She organized them in neat stacks, making certain that there were no wrinkles in them as she laid them in her dresser drawers. She smiled, liking the smell of the detergent she had used on them, the way the stacks lay in their orderly rows.

She smiled when she was certain that everything was in its place. She didn't feel as out of control when everything was in order. She let out a sigh, turning off the light and walking to the living room.

Mase grinned at her, completely back to normal since they were in his safe place. "Mom called. She said her flight got delayed, so she's not going to be back until tomorrow night. She says me and her should go shopping again, 'cause she doesn't think Bruce has good taste in clothes."

Jade rolled her eyes. "Dad has good taste in clothes and I think your clothes are great."

"Me too! Bruce just laughed. He thought it was funny. He told Mom that he was a little boy once."

"No he was not," she said with a laugh. "Dad was born just as he is now. I don't care what his mom says."

Mase chuckled, his head tipped to the side. "What do you think I'll be like when I grow up?"

She gave him a considering look, then smiled. "I think you'll be tall and strong, because you're already filling out, looking less skinny and more muscly than you did just a few months ago." She tapped her chin. "I think you'll be a basketball player. I think you'll be one of those guys that never gets a big head, the kind that talks about how if it wasn't for your coach, your team, you'd be nothing. I like those players."

Mase grinned. "Cool. If I get to be a basketball player, will you come and watch me play?"

"Are you kidding? I'll come to every game, no matter where it is. I'll start a fan club for you and wave gigantic signs that say 'Go Mase, Go!' and things like that."

He laughed, but it fell away quickly, a pensive look on his boyish face. "But Jade, those guys give interviews and stuff. They talk to reporters and to the camera, and there's always people all around them." He swallowed, his eyes going down in shame. "People make me not want to talk and stuff. I don't know what to say when somebody I don't know talks to me. I get - scared," he said, his cheeks flaming red.

Jade knelt down on the ground in front of him. "You don't have to be scared of anything or anyone, Mase. I'll keep you safe and I'll make sure you always know what to say when you get famous. I promise you, Mase."

Bruce stepped into the room, his expression cold, something utterly unfamiliar to both. "Will you two do me a favor and go outside for a while?" he asked quietly, his face haggard.

"What's wrong, Dad?" Jade asked.

"Go please, Jade. Just go," he said and sat down on the couch, looking to be on the verge of tears.

Mase walked over and laid his hand over Bruce's. "I hope you feel better," he said, going to change his clothes.

"Dad, please tell me what's wrong," Jade said, twisting her hands while she stared at him.

"Nothing, Jade. I just don't feel well. I'm going to lie down for a little while," he said, his eyes not meeting hers.

She swallowed, aware that was not the truth, but seeing that he would not speak of the thing that afected him in such a way.

Chapter 8

"Don't let a cruel word escape your mouth.
There is no greater sin than breaking a
heart."

Kamand Kojouri

The Present

Declan pulled up in front of a charming, ranch-style house in Chapel Hill. The trees around the area made the house even more picturesque. It looked like the perfect place, not too affluent, not too modest, a comfortable and inviting home.

He got out of his car and walked up to the door, smiling when he heard a booming bark from behind the door. Again, it seemed only right, the perfect sound to come from such a house. He pressed his finger to the doorbell and grinned as the dog scrabbled at the door sounding big enough to knock the door down.

"Sit, Fletch," came a man's voice from behind the door just seconds before it was opened. "Can I help you?" Bruce asked, his face tired and haggard, his gray hair, and the deep furrows around his eyes making him appear twice the age Declan knew him to be.

"Are you Bruce Rosenberg?"

He nodded.

"I'm Declan Burke."

Bruce nodded again. "Mase called me, told me to expect you. Come - no, let's go outside," he said quietly, snapping his fingers to get the dog to follow him.

Fletch barked joyfully and dashed past Bruce to sniff at Declan's pants.

Declan chuckled, kneeling down to pet the dog. "He's an Otterhound, isn't he?"

Bruce leaned inward. "A hundred and ten pounds of water loving fur," he said, a small smile coming to him as the dog ran out toward the pond as though to prove his point.

Declan stood and looked at the man, seeing the sweat on his brow and the skin that was bunched around his eyes. "Been an awful week for you," he said with compassion.

Bruce sniffed. "Ronnie tells me you were once a cop, that you still have connections in the police department. Were they able to tell you anything or are they still convinced that she did this herself?"

"They're looking into it."

"They looked into it last week and told me that my daughter was merely trying to--" he slumped into a chair, his palms pressed into his eyes. "I already told the cops, so I imagine you know what I said to her two days before she disappeared."

Declan nodded.

"I can't even tell you why I said that to her. I've never doubted that she was my daughter, even though Lindy cheated on me." He stopped, tears gleaming in his eyes. "I have made many, many mistakes in raising my daughter, but the two biggest were not telling her the day her mom was released from the nursing home, then telling her last week that I had lied to her for years. I wish I could say that I had her best interests at heart, but the truth is, I didn't want to deal with her reaction to the news all those years ago. She reacted much differently than I imagined she would. She just gave me a look of incredible pain - and walked away from me. She just walked away from me and now - I don't even know if she's alive."

"Did you talk to her after that day?" Declan asked in a calm, quiet voice.

Bruce shook his head. "I thought she just needed time to cool of. I thought she'd just come back, tell me what a jerk I was, and we'd go back to nomal."

"What would have been her nomal reaction?"

He let out a hollow laugh. "She's been a hot-head since she could talk. Piss her off and she'd tear you a new one, but she never held a grudge. After she'd said what she needed to say to clear the mad from her mind, she'd let it go, or I always thought she did. I keep going over the old days, seeing things I don't even know if they're true or my imagination. I'm beginning to think that she never really let go of her pain. I think she pushed it aside because she needed love so badly. She'd let go enough so that you couldn't see it, but her eyes always told the truth."

"Mr. Rosenberg, do you believe your daughter held a grudge, made it appear that someone had kidnapped her just to cause those who had hurt her as much pain as she could?"

Bruce shook his head. "No, I don't. She was never a liar. She'd tell the truth no matter what. Honest to a fault, my Jade."

"What do you believe happened?" Declan asked, holding the man's gaze.

"I do not know. That note said that they would make demands, but no one has contacted me, Mase or Ronnie. If it was a ransom they were after, they should have contacted us. I - I just don't know," he said in a weak voice.

Declan waited for a moment to allow the man to collect himself before he pressed on in his investigation. "Can I ask you about your first wife?"

"What about her?"

"How long were you married?" Declan asked in a voice that did not judge, a voice that understood.

Bruce sighed. "Lindy and I got married a couple years after college. Before she started showing symptoms, she was this passionate woman who would have done anything for anyone who was in need. I noticed a few strange things, like how she'd move more slowly than usual or her hands would shake. I didn't realize what it meant, and I don't think she knew either. After Jade was born, it was like a switch was flipped. Lindy went from the beautiful, funny, clever woman she had been to an obsessive psycho that would wake me up in the night, screaming that the baby was evil, that she was raped by the devil, that God had told her that the child was the antichrist," he ran his hand over his eyes yet again. "I thought at first that she might be schizophrenic, but the doctor said that sometimes, with Huntington's, it changes the mind as much as it changes the body." He cringed. "I didn't know how bad it was at first. I would notice marks on Jade, but I never thought Lindy would hurt her I was so stupid. So blind. Jade would tell me sometimes how she was wicked, but it didn't really register in my head. I was so focused on myself, how my wife's condition was affecting me, I didn't even think about what it was doing to my daughter." A tear rolled down the man's cheek and dripped onto the porch unheeded before he went on. "When Jade was seven, Lindy set the house on fire, tied my little girl to her bed, and slit Jade's wrists. She sat there to watch as the evil left. If I had got home one minute later Jade would have died. It was a near thing

103

even then. She was in the hospital for weeks, scared to death, thinking she was evil. She honestly believed she had brought evil into the world." He stopped, turning to look at Declan. "I vowed to love and cherish my wife until death, but I couldn't do it. I hated myself for being so blind, and I even hated my daughter sometimes. I divorced Lindy and never even went to visit her I couldn't stand the sight of her anymore."

Declan didn't speak. He watched like a movie played in his mind while the man described what their life had been like, and it made his heart ache for all of them.

Bruce swallowed and rubbed tiedly at his eyes. "Why am I telling you all this?" he asked with a humorless laugh.

"Maybe it was just time to talk about it. Maybe you needed to tell someone that you don't know," Declan said, the quiet compassion in his voice something that seemed to pod Bruce on.

He sighed. "Maybe so." He leaned his head back in his chair and stared up at the roof of the porch. "Jade forgot a lot of it, or maybe she just pushed it aside so that she could function. I don't even know. She'd wake up at night, about once a month screaming, thinking the house was on fire. She thought she had brought hell to earth. That was one of Lindy's little delusions that she infected Jade with." He stopped when a car pulled into the driveway. Both men rose as they saw Mase stumbling from the car, moving at a breakneck speed toward the house.

Bruce ran to him, coming to a skidding halt in front of him, reaching out to steady them both. "Tell me. What is it?" he asked before Mase could say a word.

"They - found a woman - in the Neuse River. Been there - a week or so. They--" his voice broke, tears in his eyes as Bruce's knees buckled, taking him down to the ground as though all hope had gone from him.

Declan pulled out his cell phone, dialing the number he knew so well.

"What?"

"Frank, what's up?" he asked, hoping beyond hope that the news would be different than it seemed.

"I've got problems here, Decs. Can you just tell me what you're looking for?" Frank snapped in his usual harassed way.

"The woman that was found in the river, I'm here with Bruce Rosenberg and Mase DaCosta. I need to know if it's Jade."

"No Decs, it's not her It's a black woman in her forties. Tell that kid to turn off his scanner and let us call him if we find anything," Frank harrumphed and ended the call.

Declan stepped forward and knelt down next to Bruce. "Mr Rosenberg, it's not Jade. It's okay. It's not her" he said, seeing that he had not even heard the words. "Mr. Rosenberg, it's not Jade," he said more forcefully.

Mase stared at him. "Are you sure? I

heard them talking about it, I heard them."

Declan shook his head. "I'm positive."

Bruce's eyes came up, a look mingling with both sorrow and joy. "Please, help me find my little girl. I have to find her. I can't do this again. I can't take this," he said in a weak voice.

Declan nodded. "I am going to do everything in my power to help you find the truth, Mr. Rosenberg. I can't guarantee you good news, but I can promise you the truth."

Bruce rose, the weight he bore seeming to have aged him ten years in the last few minutes, but his stance was firm. "I don't know if you're just playing me to get the story or if you really do care, but at this point, I don't care. If you really can give me the truth, I will give you the story. I'll sign whatever papers you need if you can just give me that truth." He held out his hand to shake.

Declan took the man's hand and shook it soberly.

Bruce put his hand on Mase's shoulder and walked back to the house, beckoning for Declan to follow.

Fletch bounded from the water, shaking himself vigorously, then ran at top speed toward the three men.

Mase sniffed, smiling just slightly, kneeling down to run his hand over the dog's wet fur. "We're going to find her. We will find her, Fletch."

The dog barked at the sound of his name, looking around as though it confused him why he saw Bruce and Mase, but not Jade.

They walked into the house and it was as though Mase and Bruce shrank. Their shoulders slumped and their eyes turned down, even their walks changing. It was like they both felt the weight of Jade's gaze bearing down on them from the photos on the walls. Their responsibility, whether it was imagined or deserved, weighed heavily on them.

Declan looked around with interest, his attention caught by a photo of a dark-haired girl with creamy skin and flashing green eyes. He knew that this must be Jade, and his heart skipped a beat. He had seen her many times, but had never known her name. She often came into the news stations with various clients, her smile something that captivated, but her eyes, as Bruce had alluded to, always told the truth.

She was a woman who exuded beauty and self-possession. Her eyes spoke of the doubt, of a longing for love that had never been fulfilled, of her sorow and a near bitterness at the life she had been forced to live. Her eyes were indeed honest to a fault. Rage shone though one picture in particular, her eyes fixed on Bruce and a woman that was obviously Mase's mother.

"You look surprised," Bruce said from his side.

Declan nodded. "I've seen her at the news stations."

His mouth quirked into a small smile. "I think she was born a publicist. When she told me that's what she intended to do with her life, I told her I had known that since she was five and started a fight with a little boy in the playground because he said that his dad could beat me up."

Declan chuckled, turning to look at the man. "Mr. Rosenberg, I need you to be truly honest with me no matter how it looks, no matter how you feel, I need to know the truth. Why did you tell your daughter that you had doubts as to her being yours?"

Bruce's eyes moved to a photo on the mantle of Jade, her eyes fixed on some spot over the picture taker's shoulder. She looked to be on the verge of tears. It was a beautiful picture, showing off all of her loveliest features, but her eyes, oh the story they told. "She came over - to tell me she had contacted her mother that they had planned to meet. She wasn't angry like I thought she would be, she just told me this, watching me like she expected me to attack her. I'm very much afraid of what Lindy said to her. She had a way of twisting facts to make herself the victim." He swallowed, his eyes still fixed on the photo. "I did attack. I went for the place that I knew would hurt her most. I gave her doubt that I was even her father I have no excuses, I have no reasons why I was right. I was angry, so I swung hard."

"Why?"

"I wanted for her to fight me. I wanted for her to react as her mother would have done, so that I could just - write her off." He swallowed and dropped his chin to his chest. "I knew when I saw the tears in her eyes that I had made the kind of mistake that would ruin everything. I knew she would never forgive me."

Declan sighed as he pulled away

from the house a few hours later It was amazing to him how the men that wee now so ardently looking for Jade had been so unconcerned about her just a few days before she had gone missing. A kernel of doubt filled his mind, wondering if the need to escape would have made her disappearance look to be the work of another.

He ran his hand over his eyes and shook his head. "So you leave your dad's house, your heart aching, your hand resting on your stomach whee you know the new life is growing. You'd wonder if bringing a child into the world you live in, would be fair. You'd wonder if, since your dad may not even be your dad, the only love you've ever really known, you'd wonder if it was even possible that Ronnie would stand by his child." His mind showed him the woman as she dove away from the house and his heart went out to her.

He picked up his cell phone, gritting

his teeth as he dialed the number

"Hello?"

"What did you say to her to break it off?" Declan asked without preamble.

Ronnie sighed. "Decs, I--"

"Answer the question."

He huffed out a breath. "I told her it would never work. I told her I didn't want to be a father. I told her to have an abortion and forget that any of it ever happened."

"How did she react? What did she say? What were her words, as exactly as you can remember them?" He put the phone on speaker and turned on his recording app.

"She just looked at me for a long time, then nodded and stood up. 'I will never kill anything or anyone. There will be no abortion. No matter what it takes, no matter what it costs me, I will be different.' Then she walked out. I kind of lost it. I ran after her" He cleared his throat. "She looked at me like she would have liked nothing better than to run me over. She shook her head, pulling her arm away and got into her car That was exactly seven days ago at eight o'clock tonight."

"Did you try to call her, go by to see her, anything?" Declan asked, sharply.

"No. I went home and got drunk."

"You sure?"

"I didn't go home alone. We both got drunk and--"

"Her name."

"Heather."

Declan rolled his eyes. "Last?"

Ronnie sighed. "I don't know. I was feeling pretty bad and went up to the bar to have a drink, try to brace myself before I went over to talk to Jade. Heather was just there. Gorgeous woman and she--"

"You stupid little punk. Did you tell this to the cops?" Declan asked though his teeth.

"Wha - why am I stupid for--"

"She was there to keep you from

going to Jade's house. You played right into their hands. If Jade is dead, her blood is on your hands." he snapped, hanging up before Ronnie could respond.

Chapter 9

"All things truly wicked start from innocence."

Ernest Hemingway

Fourteen Years Ago

Jade beamed as Bruce, Mase, and Portia walked into the dining room, Bruce carrying a cake on a large plate. "Happy Birthday to you. Happy Birthday to you. Happy Birthday dear Jade. Happy Birthday to you," they sang and set the cup of fruit down in front of her.

"Are you one? Are you two?" Mase began, grinning widely.

Jade laughed. "Let me stop you before you get higher than you can count. I'm fifteen, Mase. Three more years and I'm free," she said with a snide smirk at Bruce.

He chuckled. "Free to go out into the real world and discover why adults wish they were children all over again." He motioned to the cup in front of her. "Now blow out those candles before you end up with waxed fruit," he said, lifting his camera to take her picture as she blew them out.

Laughter filled the house as Bruce set a cupcake down in front of Mase and Portia while he and Jade both had cups of fruit. It was as though they were a family for the first time, a real family whose only concern was for the joy of the others. They laughed and smiled, enjoying the time together, the camaraderie.

When they had finished their cake, Mase jumped up from his chair and ran into the other room. He came back a moment later with a prettily wrapped box.

"This is from me!" he shouted and set the box on the table.

Jade leaned forward and kissed Mase's forehead. "You are the best there is," she proclaimed, her smile wide and sweet.

He shook his head. "Open it before you tell me how cool I am. You don't even know if I'm cool yet." He beamed and sat down next to her, his eyes alight while he watched her.

Jade found the edge of the wrapping paper and eased the tape away. She turned the box, doing the same to the other side, then flipped it onto its top. She found the tape and carefully slit it.

"Come on, Jade! Just rip it and see what I got you - with my own money - and a little of Bruce's."

She shook her head and took the paper from the box, then neatly folded it and set it aside.

She went through the same process with the box, carefully, oh so carefully slitting the tape. After what felt like hours, the box was open and she looked down at a pair of wireless headphones. She looked up at Mase with a smile. "Now can I say that you're the best?"

He chuckled. "Okay, now I am the best, but Bruce paid for some of it, so he can be cool too," Mase said generously, beaming at them all as Jade took the headphones from the box.

She chuckled. "Mase, it is the coolest present. I love it. You know what this means though, don't you?"

"What?"

"Since Dad's not going to be bellowing at me to turn my music down anymore, you need to start blasting your music. We wouldn't want him to be too comfortable, would we?" she asked, grinning at Bruce.

Mase nodded. "Awesome! I'll start now!"

"Hold on, Mase. There's other presents too," Bruce said with a grin, handing a cheery gift bag over to her

Jade smiled, lifting the tissue paper from the bag and folding it as always before she set it atop the papers from Mase's box. As she put her hand back into the bag, her eyes met Bruce's and she could see that his brows were drawn together, but she could not understand why as she lifted out a small box.

"It's an heirloom - your first," Bruce said in a small voice.

Jade looked at the box for a long moment, then lifted the lid to find a silver cross with a diamond set in the center She opened her mouth in shock as she looked at her dad. "But I'm only fifteen. Aren't you supposed to get heirlooms when you're eighteen or twenty-one?"

He swallowed, shifting around in his seat. "I just wanted for you to have it now."

She looked down at the cross, then back at her dad, a lump in her throat. "I don't understand. Who is this from?" she asked, her hands sweaty while her heart pounded out an irregular rhythm.

Portia threw her hands up. "I'd say that a thank you might be more in order than badgering him with questions," she snapped.

Jade ignored her, again looking at the cross, tears gleaming in her eyes. "Why are you giving this to me, Dad?"

Bruce stood and walked to where she sat. He knelt down and rested his hand over hers. "It was blessed by a priest," he said, not meeting her eyes. "You should wear it."

Fire. Blood. Screaming. Pain. They were all there inside her. The images fought to be free, fought to take control of her.

The table vibrated. The stack of papers shifted. Her wrists throbbed with remembered pain.

No. No. No. I'm not wicked. I'm not!

Portia let out a shriek and skittered away from the table, her hand pressed to her throat while she watched those things move.

Mase didn't react at all, though neither did Bruce. They watched her their expressions of nothing but trust and love.

Jade tried to clear the images from her mind. Her head throbbed with pain as her wrists ached. "Thank you," she said in a robotic tone, leaning forward to hug him.

He still didn't look at her "You're welcome," he said, unhooking the clasp of the necklace and putting it around her neck.

Jade held her breath as the cross touched her skin. She expected it to scorch her skin like a vampire in the movies, though her skin remained unmarked. The only discomfort she felt was in her lungs.

She took a deep breath and let it out slowly. She was okay. Everything was okay. She could breathe again.

She gave him a hesitant smile as she carefully began unwrapping the next present.

When she had finished unwrapping the presents from Bruce, of which there were quite a number, Jade hugged her dad again. "I don't get you, Dad. Why do you spend so much money on birthdays when you know I'd be just as happy with a hug and a 'Happy Birthday'?"

He chuckled and hugged her close.

"It's a bribe. I buy you the presents to try to keep you little."

Jade laughed. "I'll consider your bribe, but I don't think it'll work."

Portia sighed and pushed a gift bag toward Jade. "It doesn't seem that you need anything else, but that one is fom me," she said, pouring another shot of Vodka into her lemonade.

Jade raised her brows. "Thanks," she said with as little enthusiasm as Portia had shown. She reached into the bag which had no tissue paper of any kind and took out a makeup kit. She looked at it, then looked at Portia.

"It's makeup, Jade. You've been old enough to wear it for a while now and since you might want to date at some point," she said, pouring herself yet another drink.

Bruce scowled at his wife. "Now that is the kind of thing I'm hoping to avoid. Jade can't date, ever" He pointed a finger at Jade. "You're going to be my little girl for the rest of your life."

She grinned, exhausted from pretending that everything was okay. She offered her hand to Mase. "Come on, Mase-Man, let's see what Dad thinks when we blast your music loud enough to shake the walls." She picked up her gifts, her throat feeling tight as the cross around her neck grew warm.

As she and Mase walked back to her bedroom, a lightness filled Jade's chest when she heard Bruce's voice pitched low, asking Portia what her problem was. Her smile became wide while the tension in her body eased. For the first time in longer than she could remember, she felt that her life was hopeful, right, maybe even good.

Chapter 10

"Keep a little fire burning; however small,
however hidden."

Cormac McCarthy

The Present

Declan did a double take when he pulled up in front of the building that housed the publicity firm where Jade worked. It was not what he had expected. The building itself was ostentatious, its mirored facade and ornate sculptures standing out in a way that he found annoying for a eason he couldn't identify.

He shook the feeling of while he parked and walked up to the building. He needed a clear mind. He knew the questions he wanted to ask and the things he needed to see. It was time to see what other truths Jade Rosenberg would reveal to him.

He stepped through the glass front doors of the building and smiled pleasantly at the man behind the counter "Could I speak with Juan Flores?"

The man tapped his fingers on the desk. "Do you have an appointment?" he asked, as though he accused Declan of something heinous.

"I do. I'm Declan Burke."

The receptionist picked up the phone. "Mr. Flores, your one o'clock appointment is here, fifteen minutes early," he said and listened for a moment, then hung up the phone. "He'll be down in a minute," he said, turning back to his computer with a scowl.

Declan tried not to laugh, but had to bite the inside of his cheek to prevent that sound from escaping him. He walked to one of the enormous windows and organized the questions in his mind.

"Mr. Burke?" a voice said from behind him.

Declan turned and smiled, offering his hand. The man was nearing sixty, though could have passed for several years younger if his expression had not been so strained. "It's Declan, Mr Flores."

He nodded as he shook Declan's hand. "I'm Juan. You work for channel five, don't you? The reporter who does the investigative stories? They've been calling you the channel five bluecoat."

Declan shrugged deprecatingly. "That's really not accurate, Juan. I work with a team and we make no arrests, we just tell the stories and then hand our evidence over to the authorities."

He clicked his tongue with a small smile. "That's the thing you expect to hear from a reporter. Just say thank you and let it pass."

Declan chuckled, walking with the man toward the elevator. "Thank you," he said.

As the elevator door closed, Juan turned to look at him. "You're here about Jade?" he asked in a rush.

"I'm looking into the story of her disappearance. I've been asked to help find her," he said, watching the man's face to see his reaction.

Juan sighed in a relieved way. "She is an amazing publicist, makes her clients appear to be her best friend, makes everyone appear to be her best friend, but I don't know a soul who could tell you a thing about her personal life."

"Could you?" Declan asked, his voice one of compassion, no condemnation.

He shrugged. "As much as she would allow me to know. She's a painfully private person, but somehow people feel close to her, love her. The office has been miserable since last Wednesday. No one seems to know what to do."

It surprised Declan when he and Juan exited the elevator to find disconsolate faces all around, not a single smile brightening the area. He wondered if such an attitude was put on, or if the woman had made such a diference to the morale of the office.

He had grown used to having to wade through the way people wanted a person to be perceived and the truth. What he saw seemed to be true grief, a genuine remorse that Jade was not with them.

They walked through the area to an office with the nameplate, 'Rosenbeg' written rather cheerlessly on the door He smiled as they walked into the ofice, seeing that it was painfully neat, not a single paper out of place. Despite that, there was an inviting quality to it. Thee were a few pictures on the walls, one of which caught his eye, making him walk over to look more closely at it.

Juan chuckled. "That is the only part of this office that I never understood. It seems so out of character but she never explains why it's there."

Declan's stomach balled into a tight knot at the thought of Jade keeping such a thing around herself, as though in punishment or reminder, he did not know.

It was a painting of a dark night, but a fire blazed, burning all in its path. A dark form stood, staring at the flames, either mesmerized or fear struck. This painting gave him a glimpse into the woman's heart, a mere glimpse at the way she struggled daily to fight the past and embrace the future.

The desk was empty of all clutter, its only adornments a lamp, a phone, and a sculpture of a hand. He had guessed the space would be clean, though he hadn't expected it to be so empty. Minimalism appeared to be her life's philosophy.

Declan turned to look at Juan, seeing the man's eyes fixed on the desk as though he could see Jade behind it. "When was the last time you saw Jade?" he asked in a quiet tone while he turned on the recording app on his phone. He did his best not to break the thread of the man's thoughts with any abrupt movement or question.

Juan swallowed. "Just over a week ago, at lunch on Monday. She got this call and left the office." He swallowed again. "I didn't think to ask where she was going, she's such a good publicist, brings in more clients than the rest of my staff put together. I just thought she had a new client or something." He ran his hand over his face. "I'm pretty sure something was wrong, though. Now that I look back, I wish I would have asked her where she was going, but I didn't bother I just watched her get into the elevator It was like she wasn't there, like only her body moved, but her heart, her soul was just gone from her. She had appointments all day on Tuesday, so she didn't come into the office." He let out a tired sigh.

"I can get a subpoena for the phone records, see what the call was, that's not a problem. Are you certain that she gave you no sign of who had called her or where she was going?"

Juan shook his head. "Nothing. She looked scared, though. Why didn't I stop her, make her tell me where she was going? She was even walking strangely,

133

her briefcase over her shoulder but she walked with her hands covering her wrists. That was very much not like her.' He looked at the chair again, his shoulders slumped like that tale had wilted him.

Declan groaned inwardly, knowing where she had gone and why. "I had hoped to interview your staf today, Juan, but there's something I need to check out. Do you mind if I come back?"

He shook his head, his eyes still fixed on the chair.

Declan let out a slow breath as he got into his car, shaking his head in wonder as he pulled out his phone.

"What?" Frank snapped into the phone.

"So what if I was the Commissioner just looking for an update on how you're doing?" he asked with a small smile.

Frank snorted. "The Commissioner doesn't have your ringtone. What do you want, Declan?"

"I need Jade's mother's name, address too if you want to give it. I'm thinking Jade went to see her mom on the Monday before she disappeared, and if she did, that explains a lot."

Frank made a clicking noise. "I'll give you the address if you work with me on this one, Decs. If that girl didn't just run off, my case needs help."

"Okay, man. Meet me at Jade's townhouse in an hour and bring that address," he said, ending the call before Frank could respond.

He looked at the time on his phone, realizing he had not eaten since the oatmeal at around four o'clock that morning. He had gotten by on cigarettes and coffee. He began driving, his mind still stuck on the painting of fire.

"So you keep it close to you to remind you of who you are, what you've come from, but it's also as a reminder to you not to let anyone in. You don't let anyone see anything more than the surface. You hide behind your interest in other people's lives. You know so much about everyone, but make certain that they know nothing of you," he vocalized, seeing the form of Jade, in the passenger seat next to him, nodding in agreement. "So that Monday, you're in your office. It's a place that has always been safe for you and you get a call from the past, one you can't hide from. It brings back every fear you've ever had. Why did you go to meet her, Jade? Why would you put yourself through that?" he asked, desperate to find an answer to that question.

He went to one of his favorite cofee shops and ordered his lunch. When that was done, he sat at a table and took out his laptop, making detailed notes of everything that Juan had told him. He highlighted Juan's name so he would not forget how many questions he had for the man, how many clarifications he wanted made.

Were they sleeping together? Had

they at one time? Was it a simple infatuation that made the older man speak with such longing for Jade?

He stared at his computer for a long moment, then looked up, smiling as a young server brought over his lunch. He took a bite of his sandwich, then set it down again. Something bothered him about the office, though he could not identify what it was.

He felt certain that he had been lied to. He knew it as certainly as he knew Jade had to be found as soon as humanly possible. Her life hung in the balance. If she was not dead, she soon would be. He had to find her, had to get to the bottom of the story.

He picked up his sandwich again, grimacing as his cell phone rang. He answered it without bothering to look at the display. "Yeah," he said through a mouthful of food.

"Hi," a childish voice said, sounding utterly disconsolate.

"Hey, Sean. What are you doing?" he asked with a smile as he took another bite of his sandwich.

"Nothing. Dad, can I come and live with you?" the little boy asked in a rush.

Declan raised his brows. "What's going on, buddy? Why are you asking me this?"

Sean sniffled into the phone. "Jacob's mean, I don't want to live here anymore."

Declan leaned back in his chair grinning at the sandwich in his hand. "How is Jacob mean?"

Sean sniffed. "He spanked my butt."

"Uh huh, what for?"

The little boy paused, not answering the question.

Declan continued to eat. "What did you do, Sean?"

He sniffed again. "I kicked him."

"Why did you kick Jacob?"

"Well - I don't know. Mommy didn't yell at him or nothing when he spanked me. It hurt too."

Declan grinned, taking a quick drink of his coffee. "Sean, you can't go around kicking people when you feel like it, you know that. Jacob didn't do anything that I wouldn't have done if I was there. And you know Mom knows best, right?"

"I guess," he grumbled.

"Did you tell Jacob that you were sorry you kicked him?"

"No."

"I think you should, buddy. He's a really good guy, and he makes your mom happy. That means a lot to me."

"But Dad, does that mean I can't come and live with you?" he whined.

"The way things are now work out so well for you and me, Sean. I'm gone all the time, but when we have our weekends together, I can take the whole time to spend with you. Why don't you talk to Jacob and your mom and just see what you think next week?"

"Okay, I think mom wants to talk to you," he grumbled.

"Alright. I'll talk to you soon," Declan said, taking another quick bite of his sandwich as he gathered the rest of his things up so he would not miss his appointment with Frank.

"Decs?" a husky voice asked into the phone.

"What's going on, April?" Declan said, picking up his cofee and taking it with him as he exited the store.

"Just wanted to see how you're doing. Your story last week was very interesting."

"Glad you watched, thanks," he said, pulling out onto the road while he waited to see why she was buttering him up.

"Decs, I need to ask a favor"

"Ask away, babe," he said, grimacing as he realized what he had said.

"Well, Jacob and I have been wanting to go away by ourselves. I was

140

just wondering if you could take Sean for ten days."

"When?" he asked, wishing fervently that he had not picked up the phone.

"Well - tomorrow."

Declan let out a small laugh, driving a little faster than he did before. "You really give me time to prepare, don't you?"

"I tried to get my parents to watch him, but they don't really want to talk to me at this point."

"Why?" he asked as he turned into Jade's neighborhood.

April let out a small laugh. "Because I walked out on the great Declan Burke, why else?"

"That has nothing to do with them."

She let out a weary sigh. "Just answer the question, Decs. Will you take Sean?"

"When have I ever said no to you, April? I'm working on a big story, so I'm not going to be around as much as he'd like. My parents would love hanging out with him while I'm--"

"Why have you never said no to me?" she asked in a rush.

He huffed, annoyed with himself for being the doormat his friends accused him of being with her. "When are you dropping Sean off?"

April didn't ask her question again. "Can I drop him off in a couple of hours?" she asked in a distracted tone.

"You can. What time do I need to be home?"

"Three would be fine. Thank you, Decs."

He grimaced. "You're welcome. See you later," he said,, ending the call as he pulled up in front of Jade's townhouse.

He stared at the building for a long moment, even more certain that he had missed something. He did his best to shrug off the old resentments while he got out of the car and walked up to the townhouse. He knelt down in the grass to look up, that movie playing in his mind.

How was it that even in the middle of the night, a man could pull into a driveway, walk up to a door, crash in, have a monumental fight, then walk out with her without being noticed?

"Anything in the grass?" Frank asked.

Declan shook his head and stood up. "Nothing, just more questions. Frankie, there's so many twists in this story I don't even know where to begin looking for her."

He nodded. "I've been going over my evidence and still, there's nothing."

"If the mother knows anything, anything at all, how likely is it she'll tell us?"

"Not likely at all. She hates cops. Wouldn't even let us in the door when we came by to tell her that her daughter was missing and spit at me when I came back to see if she would talk to me."

Declan raised his brows. "Then why are you coming with me? If she--"

"Because if that girl is dead, it is my responsibility to find her, to find who and to find why. I can't do that by standing back and letting some reporter take all my glory," he growled.

Declan merely stood, continuing to stare at the townhouse.

"So what else is on your mind?" Frank asked.

"I've got Sean for ten days, probably more, knowing April. I kind of have a bad feeling, like she's planning not to come back."

Frank laid his hand on his friend's shoulder. "Declan, she shouldn't be raising your boy, anyway. Yes, you loved her. Her little fling with Jacob will last a year or so, then she'll come crawling back to you, begging you to forgive her for being a cheating whore. You had better not, Declan. Stand up, take your son and make your life." He turned away and stomped back to his car

Chapter 11

"If it doesn't challenge you, it won't change you."

Fred DeVito

Thirteen Years Ago

"You're a good runner," a voice said from Jade's side as she ran through the woods, most of the cross-country team far behind her.

"Thanks," she said dismissively, picking up her pace.

She knew he was the guy she'd seen at the mall over the summer, although she wasn't in the mood to deal with him. All she wanted was to run. Running faster and further than anyone else had been the highlight of her year.

Todd chuckled. "Seriously, are you ever friendly?" he asked, remaining by her side with ease.

"Sometimes," she said shortly.

"Okay, like when?"

Jade continued running, trying to pretend that she had heard nothing from the boy who ran beside her

After a while, Todd sent her a challenging grin. "I'll make you a deal. If you can beat me to the finish line, I'll leave you alone completely, won't talk to you ever again. But if I win, you go on a date with me."

Jade ran on, her ponytail swinging in time with the motion of her run.

"Scared?"

She rolled her eyes. "No, I'm not."

"Well?" he asked.

Jade nodded. "Deal," she said and took off, much faster than seemed even possible.

Todd picked up his pace as well, allowing her to stay only a small length in front of him.

Jade enjoyed the challenge, aware that he toyed with her, but she didn't particularly care. She smiled as the woods cleared and the open field in front of them led to the finish line spread out in front of her. She knew Todd would put on a burst of speed, planning to pass her, but she maintained her pace, a small smile playing around her mouth.

As Todd extended his stride, she did the same, her body working harder than she had ever made it work. Her legs were screaming, but she forced herself to go harder and faster than ever As they reached the finish line, she put on one last burst of speed, reaching the finish line at the exact second that Todd reached it. They tied for first place, a thing that shocked even her.

She slowed, feeling her legs quiver in protest. Her hands shook and her lungs screamed. She was not at all certain that she had not injured herself, but right then, she did not care. She felt a surge of pride, pure, simple pride that he had not beaten her.

"Holy cow," Todd said, puffing for breath as they jogged to cool down, then slowed to a walk. "I never thought you could do that," he panted, fighting for his own breath.

Jade nodded, unable to articulate a thought, let alone gather enough breath to speak.

"So uh, can I still ask you out?" he asked, as her eyes turned up to meet his.

A small smile came to Jade's lips, but she shook her head. She gulped in one last breath, then stopped to stretch. "That wasn't the deal."

Todd shifted uncomfortably and tugged on his ear. "What's wrong with going on a date? We could just go to a movie or something, go with some people, I don't care."

Jade shook her head. "I can't. I just can't. I'm just not interested in dating."

"Why?"

Because I'm wicked. She shook that thought off. "Because I'm not interested in being seen. I just want to be left alone," she told him, the ache in her heart something that almost made her weep.

She so desperately wanted to be

seen. She wanted to do something, anything other than deal with the power that felt so impossible to contol. What she was, what she came fom meant that she would be alone foever.

"Jade!" a jubilant voice called and Mase launched himself forwad, hugging her tightly. "That was so cool, Jade! You were so fast!" he shouted, clearly too excited even to recall his fear of crowds.

She grinned as she looked aound for her dad. She narowed her eyes when she saw that Bruce stood back, giving Todd a look that a hungry lion would give to a gazelle; on alert, ready to pounce. She stepped towad him with Mase, her fingers tingling as she looked at her dad. "I didn't know you guys were coming," she said, a shiver passing over her skin as his eyes met hers.

"Mase didn't want to miss it," he said in a crisp voice, folding his ams over his chest. "We'll wait by the car and you can finish here."

Jade shook her head. She raised her chin and squared her shoulders, ignoring the adrenaline that pulsed through her body. "All I have to do is tell my coach I'm riding back with you," she said, and turned her back on him to walk toward her coach.

"Jade, how come you and Bruce are mad?" Mase asked, still by her side.

She sighed and put her arm over his shoulders. "Because Dad thinks I'm somebody that I'm not. He thinks that I'm a liar as well, I think."

Mase frowned. "But who does Bruce think you are?"

"My mom," she said in a near whisper, tears coming to her eyes at the pain of that admission. *You're a wicked girl. The devil will take you.*

Mase put his arm around Jade's waist. "Don't be sad, Jade. You're the coolest sister anybody ever had and I know who you are."

She smiled, ducking her head to

kiss his cheek. "And you're the coolest brother. Promise me you'll never change, that you'll always be the coolest guy."

He grinned and nodded. "You got a deal, but only if you promise you won't change either. Tanner wishes I would just drop off the face of the earth and he really is my brother."

Jade turned to look at him. "Listen to me, Mase. Your brother's opinion doesn't matter. You are important and you deserve to be treated like you are. He's wrong. Got me?"

He blinked. "You're important too, Jade."

Her stomach flipped, though she gave him a smile before she turned to tell her coach that she was leaving.

As she turned back to where her father stood, Jade's mouth opened in shock when she saw Todd talking to Bruce. It was a strange thing to see the two, but more strange to see Bruce's eyes meet hers, a smile on his lips.

"Bruce looks happy again," Mase observed. "That guy looks nice too, Jade. Can he be our friend?"

Jade sighed. "It doesn't look like I've got a choice," she said, a slight note of bitterness in her voice.

"I won't be his friend if you don't want me to, Jade. I'll be mad at him, just like you."

She shook her head, smiling down at the young boy with all the love she had. "You don't have to do that, Mase. Todd is a really nice guy that just doesn't know how to back off. You can be anybody's friend if I like them or not."

He shook his head. "No way. I don't want to be friends with people you don't like. I'm going to be mad at him, since he won't back off," he said, his shoulders stif under her hand, every muscle in his still skinny frame tightening as though he prepared himself for battle.

Jade chuckled. "I'm not mad at him, Mase. He really is a nice guy and I like him. Why don't we both be friends with him, okay?"

He smiled and nodded. "Cool. Want to see if he can come for one of those slushies? Me and Bruce were going to take you for one."

Jade smiled, though something caught her attention at the back of the crowd. She looked in that direction and her eyes met someone's. Her mouth fell open when her green eyes met a pair of eyes of the exact same color, someone who looked so much like her they could have been mistaken for each other under certain circumstances.

What's going on?

Chapter 12

"In a child's eyes, a mother is a goddess.
She can be glorious or terrible, benevolent
or filled with wrath, but she commands
love either way."

M.K. Jemisin

The Present

Declan's eyes widened when he and Frank pulled up in front of a house that was not at all what he had expected. The place was a modest split level, its tan siding and bold red front door complimenting the flowers in many varying shades of red, white, and blue that were scattered in flower beds throughout the yard. It looked to be a peaceful home, one that he nearly wished he had to offer his son.

He turned in his seat to look at Frank, raising his brows. "This is - pretty," he said, his bafflement showing through.

Frank scoffed. "You were expecting a rundown trailer, with bullet holes in the sides, and washing machines on the porch?"

He shrugged. "How many places have we gone to with this kind of history that were exactly like that? You can't tell me this didn't surprise you."

"I'm not telling you it didn't surprise me. I'm telling you to look past it and help me figure out if this woman killed her daughter."

Declan shook his head. "Don't go in there ready to arrest her, man. Let me do the talking and maybe you won't get spit at this time," he said, getting out of the car.

As they walked to the house, Declan's mind spun, showing him images he was not at all certain would not sway his ability to see the truth. He watched as an image of Jade came into his mind. She would have pulled into the same driveway, walked up the same path to the door of a woman who she feared more than any other. His mind watched as her hands shook, pulling the sleeves of her shirt down to cover the old scars on her wrists, the ones that could still take her back to pain and fire.

He shook his head. He needed to clear his mind. He had to focus on the moment, on finding Jade.

Declan motioned Frank back when they got to the door, knocking in a way that sounded as friendly as he could make it. He waited for only a few seconds before the door opened.

The woman who stood before them had the same basic body type as her daughter, though there was not much other resemblance between them. Lindy's hard life shone in every line on her face. The tremors of her body weren't as pronounced as he'd expected, though they were still very noticeable.

"Mrs. Grahame?" he asked in his best soothing voice.

She nodded, her eyes moving past him to where Frank stood. "I told you to stay away from here and from me," she said in a cold, hard voice.

Declan shook his head. "I'm sorry, ma'am. I asked him to come along because

158

we're both looking into the disappearance of your daughter."

"Bruce made it clear to me many years ago that the girl is no longer my daughter," she said, though she stood back, opening the screen door to allow the two into the house.

The room they stepped into was pure white. White floors. White couches. White walls. White furniture and accessories. It looked more like a clean room than a living room. And *clean room* it was. Everything spotlessly clean, like it had been organized using a slide ruler

There were a few pictures on the walls, showing a happy couple at diferent stages in their lives. It added enough color to the white space to make it almost lovely. Almost, but not quite.

"Mrs. Grahame, my name is Declan Burke. I'm a reporter, writing the story of Jade's disappearance. I would very much like to speak with you about your meeting with your daughter last Monday."

She motioned for the two men to follow her back into the kitchen where she poured three cups of coffee. She set two spotless white mugs down on the counter before them, then stood back to sip slowly at her own. Her hands had only the slightest tremors to them, but Declan could see that she'd only filled her mug half full, probably to avoid any mishap with the beverage.

She looked up from the cup she had been examining, as though it held the answers to so many secrets and met Declan's eyes. "You know that I have had - a troubled past."

He turned on his recording app and set his phone between them on the counter, taking a small drink of his cofee while he observed the woman.

"I wish I could tell you it was all untrue, but it's not. I did the things that I was accused of doing, but I'm under control now. The drugs they gave me made my symptoms less violent. They made my life liveable again. I spent my time in that hospital and they helped me. They helped me," she repeated, her eyes pleading with Declan's like she begged him to understand.

"Did Jade believe that?" he asked quietly.

She shook her head, the tears that cascaded down her cheeks only increasing. "No, she didn't." She ran a slim finger down the track of a tear "She is such a beautiful girl, so beautiful and from what I've heard, successful and good."

"What did you think of her when you saw her?"

She smiled, her hand rested on her throat. "I thought I was seeing myself twenty years ago." She snifed, an incongruous smile coming to her lips. "Sexier than I ever was, though. She wore this pretty, slim black suit, and a soft gray camisole with her hair pulled back at the base of her neck and quiet, elegant jewelry. So beautiful. So showy and classy, but her eyes - her eyes hated me. You could always see what she thought in those pretty eyes of hers, this gorgeous green color and very simple, elegant makeup that probably cost more than my entire wardrobe, but she just stood there and stared at me, the sexy little demon child. Her eyes sparkled with fire." Her voice took on a quality that was cold and frightening, no longer speaking of a beloved daughter, but a mortal enemy, a nemesis that she wished to strike down in any way she could. "She's just standing there, staring at me, and won't say a word. She won't say boo and I tell her JUST how sorry I am. I tell her JUST how proud I am of her, but she won't even bother to tell me she hates me. Her eyes say it. Satan shines through that mask she wears." Her body convulsed, a hard tremor moving over her entire body. She clenched her hands into vicious fists like she wished she could bury them in her daughter's flesh. "My son went after her He tried to talk to her, tried to tell her, but she just walked away."

"Your son?" Declan asked, his heart pounding as he watched her

She nodded. "Jade was not my first. Bruce and I got pregnant in college and I gave the baby up for adoption. He found me a few years ago and became my son yet again. He is a wonderful man. God shines through in him, not the devil, like Jade."

"What's your son's name?"

She smiled and raised her chin, a gleam in her eyes. "His name is Trenton Grahame. Sweet boy changed his name to mine when we were reunited. Good, beautiful, sweet boy," she said again, her hand pressed to her chest.

"Did you hear what they said to each other?" Declan asked, his senses singing while he took in the scene.

"I heard some of it. My son told her she owed her mother the respect that I had given her. He told her she should feel gratitude that our family was bought back together. He told her she owed her mother the life that she seemed so determined to show off. He told her she would be nothing without me."

"And what did Jade say?"

She grimaced, her cheeks flushed, her eyes snapping with a kind of light that brought on vicious storms. "She told my son that her father was all that she needed, that if it wasn't for Bruce, she would have burned alive in the house. She told him vicious lies, horrible, dark things that I know Bruce must have infected her with. She told my son that she only came here because she wanted to find a way to forget, to block me from her mind forever. Stupid girl. The devil's daughter She's not mine at all," she hissed and tears again flowed in torrents down her cheeks.

Declan wished he had his camera crew with him. The metamorphosis that had just taken place was one he could never accurately describe. The hated that radiated off the woman for her daughter was something that gave him pause.

After a moment, Lindy looked at them, her eyes red rimmed by all the tears she had cried. "I do not want that girl to be found. I want to forget that she ever existed, just as she wanted to forget me. She is not my blood." She lifted her cup to her lips and took another long drink of coffee.

Frank stepped forward. "Mrs. Grahame, I'm going to need to ask that you not leave town for any reason unless you let my office know where you have gone. The disappearance of Jade is--"

"Get out of my house," she interrupted, setting her cofee cup down with such force that it slopped onto the floor and cracked the cup in two.

"I will be back, with a warrant," Frank said and walked from the house.

Declan stayed where he was, watching as Lindy wiped the cofee up with paper towels. "Mrs. Grahame, what do you think happened to your daughter last Tuesday night?"

She scowled, picking up the pieces of the mug to set them in the garbage. She took out a mop and cleaned the floor before she deigned to speak. "I don't know. She's been dead to me for years, so what happened to her doesn't matter so much to me," she said, with a brutal honesty.

"If she was dead to you, why did you try to make contact with her?"

She sighed, leaning her head on her hands as she clasped them on the mop. "Because Trenton convinced me that children forgive, that they don't remember the things that you regret so deeply. He convinced me I could find the daughter the devil stole from me." She sniffed again and went back to the mopping of the floor "He was wrong. The girl that I gave birth to is dead, the thing that's left is a shell, hollow and repulsive."

"But you talked about how proud

you are of her," he prodded in hopes he could keep her talking.

"I was proud until I saw her" She met his eyes. "Have you seen her?"

He nodded.

"Beautiful woman, isn't she, Mr Burke?"

He nodded again.

She smiled and placed a shaky hand on her hip as she regarded him. "You're thinking that if you play knight in shining armor, rescue her from whatever dark fate she has come to, she'll take off those expensive clothes of hers for you," she said, then laughed. "Her skin is soft, supple, and those curves of hers make men want to bend her over something and pound themselves into her Hot little thing, so hot. But then, she opens her mouth and you find that there's nothing there other than a bitter and selfish whore who takes her clothes of for men that are not worthy." She smiled knowingly, leaning again on the mop. "Don't waste your time with someone like that, Mr Burke. There's more to look for in a woman than a hot body," she snarled and turned her back on him.

An odd feeling passed over Declan's skin when he walked out of the house. It wasn't the relief he'd expected to feel. Instead, it was a wary suspicion.

He'd only once before had that kind of quiver on the back of his neck. That feeling told him there was more to the story. Far more.

"Drive," Declan said the moment he got into Frank's car. He quickly dug his phone from his pocket and checked to be certain the interview was both recorded and backed up on the cloud. When he was certain of that, he played back what Lindy Grahame had just said to him.

Frank bumped his fist on the steering wheel while they listened, his teeth clenched so hard that Declan could see the muscle of his jaw bulge.

"I thought you were wrong until she

started talking." Declan rubbed his hand over his brows. "None of this makes sense. Why would she tell us how much she hates her daughter if she wanted to show us just how innocent she was?"

Frank shook his head. "Doesn't matter, Decs. The why never mattered, but you never understood that. My job is to find out who did it, not why."

He turned in his seat to look at the harsh look on his old friend's face. "If you find out why, you have the chance of stopping this kind of thing in the future."

Frank scowled. "Let's just get us some precogs in the department and stop the crimes before they even happen, Decs."

He sighed and leaned his head on his fist. "I can't go with you to talk to Trenton. I have to be back to my place before three."

"Fine," Frank snapped.

When they pulled up behind Declan's car a few minutes later Frank gave him an imperious look. "Send me a copy of that interview so I can get a warrant for that woman's arrest."

Declan raised his brows. "You're not going to get that, Frankie. She didn't say anything that will get any judge to sign off on a warrant."

"That is not your job, Declan. It's mine. I need that recording."

"Can't do it, man. It's the property of the news station, not mine. I can come in and be a witness on your behalf, but that's all I can do." Declan gathered his bag and exited the car with no further comment.

Frank got out of his car and stomped around to Declan's side, giving him the look he reserved for the most contemptible of criminals. "My goal in this is to find that girl, if nothing else, then alive. If you won't--"

"Liar," Declan snapped, his head high and his shoulders squared. "You had written her off, weren't even trying to find her until I came into this thing. The only

170

reason you're here is to make the cops look good on TV. I know the system and I know you, so don't give me your self-righteous crap. I will be a witness to the judge if you want to go over and try to get a warrant, but you will not get it on the information we got today. What we have is a mentally disturbed woman, ranting about her daughter," he spat, then shook his head before Frank could speak. "If I find anything that will help you arest that woman, I'll call," he said and walked to his car.

"Decs," Frank said, waiting as his old friend turned back to look at him. "I'll do the same for you if I find anything at the Grahame kid's place." And he got back into his car, driving away as fast as he could.

Chapter 13

"There is always a pleasure in unraveling
a mystery, in catching at the gossimer
clue which will guide to certainty."

Elizabeth Gaskell

The Present

Declan grimaced when he pulled into the parking lot of his building to find April already waiting for him. He wished she had given him a bit more time to clear his mind before taking his son. He wished that there was a way to block it out of his mind before he saw his ex-wife and her boyfriend.

He walked rather slowly toward the other while he tried to put a smile on his face. He did his best to look as though nothing was wrong.

Sean opened the back door of the car, a very grumpy look on his face. He slammed the door, then ran to Declan and threw his arms around his waist. "Mom and Jacob are being mean, Dad," he proclaimed, turning his soft blue eyes up to meet his father's, his messy brown hair

173

so like Declan's had been at his age.

"And you were just an angel, weren't you, Sean?"

He shrugged, scowling again as his mother got out of the car

"Decs," she said, stepping forward to press her lips to his cheek as she handed over Sean's bag. She stood back to look at him. "You smell like smoke and cofee. It must be a big story."

He nodded. "One of the biggest I've seen, definitely the biggest I've tried to tell."

She pushed her long, straight blonde hair back behind her ears and gave him an appraising look before she spoke. "Do you have anyone that can look after Sean while you're working?"

"I do. My sister has big plans for all of us, including something to do with all of us going to a water park on Saturday," he said, grinning down at his son.

"Cool!" Sean jumped up and down happily.

April's eyes shuttered. "I'm glad you have some plans, Decs." She laid her hand on his cheek. "You look worn out. You should do more than work and smoke, you know." Her thumb moved over his cheek as a smile played around her mouth.

Declan stepped back from her and took his son's hand. "Ten days?" he asked.

"Around that," she answered and looked at their son with a small smile, leaning down to press her lips to his forehead. "Be a good boy for your dad, alright Sean?"

He nodded. "Okay. Bye Mom," he answered with a frown.

She smiled, her eyes moving back to Declan's. "I'll see you," she said, her lips quivering.

"Have a good time, April."

She gazed at Sean before she turned away from them. "I - I will. Be happy, Decs," she said, and walked back to the car.

Declan's heart sank while he watched her drive away. His bad feeling that April may leave Sean only compounded. That had looked far more like a permanent goodbye to him than her usual short, offhand farewells.

He hoped he was doing nothing more than projecting his feelings about Jade's story onto his own life, although he didn't think so. The rift created by her relationship with Jacob had changed April. It felt almost like she'd given up, yet he didn't understand what she was giving up on.

Declan looked down at his son as the car pulled away, seeing the rather bitter look on the boy's face. "So, you planning any wild parties while you're here?"

Sean grinned and nodded. "I'm going to have all my friends over and we're going to jump on everything!"

"Everything?" he asked while he guided the boy into the apartment and handed him his bag to take back to his bedroom.

Sean nodded. "Totally everything! We're going to jump on you too, Dad!" He giggled as he ran back to his nom and tossed his bag onto his bed, then ran back at full tilt. "What story are you telling people now, Dad?" he asked eagerly.

Declan picked him up and set him on the counter. "It's a story about a little boy who's got this crazy toe that is about half an inch longer than the rest of his toes. He's on a quest to find out how to make his other toes grow to match the long one," he said with as serious an expression as he could manage.

Sean laughed and shook his head. "Liar, liar, pants on fire!" He slipped off his shoes to show his odd toe that stuck up half an inch longer than the others. "You don't tell stories about me, Dad. You tell stories about people that get hurt and then the good guys come in and save them, or sometimes you tell stories about bad people that get away and do more bad stuff, then the good guys find them and stuff."

Declan raised his brows. "Have you been watching my stories?" he asked, baffled about what April could be thinking to allow their son to see such things.

Sean nodded. "Mom don't want me to see, but Jacob says not to shelter a kid. He says that if you shelter a kid, they gow up with a small view of the world," he parroted, then squished his face into a pensive expression. "Your stories are kind of scary sometimes, but it's you, Dad. Why do I got to be scared of something you say?"

Declan shook his head. "You don't have to be afraid of anything as long as I'm around, but I don't want you watching me on the news. You get to be sheltered for a while, then I'll be the one to tell you what the world is really like, okay, buddy?"

"Okay," he said agreeably and

swung his legs happily as he looked around his father's apartment. "Can we have breakfast for supper? I want one of your cheesy ham omelettes and toast with strawberry jelly."

"Sounds good to me," he said and lifted the boy off the counter. "I need to get a little bit of work done. Do you have your thesis finished yet?"

Sean nodded soberly. "I remember that one. A thesis is a big paper that means you can get a big, important job." He rushed over to his schoolbag and took out an alphabet chart. "I'm gunna write one while you work!" and he hurried over to the coffee table to begin his writing.

Declan smiled, truly delighted by his son. But again, his mind balked at what he'd seen in Lindy Grahame's eyes. He knew his son was no angel, though even when he was downright bratty, he'd never once thought his son was evil.

The change in the way Lindy spoke about Jade was what gave him pause. It was like she spoke about a diferent person than she had at first. Could Jade have done something, or was it moe likely that Lindy's illness had caused her to react that way?

He called his producer to talk the story through, eager to see what the man would think. It was always good to get outside opinions, so he sent out all the information he'd gathered so far that day and waited.

"This is going to be big," his producer said in an awed voice.

And Declan knew it was true. They'd have to be sure to get the opinions of several doctors on how Huntington's had affected Lindy. They would have to be very careful in the way they handled that part, at least.

He set his phone down and scrubbed his hands over his face. Something about Jade's ofice continued to bother him. Could it have been Juan, or was it more likely that his eyes saw something his mind hadn't picked up on? He closed his eyes and thought back through everything he'd seen, and his certainty grew.

He'd seen something that niggled at the back of his mind. That, plus Lindy's proclamation that the devil had stolen her daughter, made him certain he overlooked something.

"Dad! I finished my thesis! Can we have supper now? I'm super hungry," Sean called excitedly.

"Uh, sure," Declan said with a smile, trying to clear the case from his mind as he walked around the bar into the kitchen.

There was a lightness in his chest at the distraction his son ofered. He knew he had to turn it off, not to allow the story to consume him. The things that Lindy had said to him rang even less true now that he saw his son. He could not comprehend any parent feeling such a bitter hatred of their child. It had been there, right there for his eyes to see.

He shook his head and took out his favorite pan, preparing the other ingredients.

"Dad, can I help?" Sean asked from his side.

Declan jerked slightly, not having heard the boy enter the kitchen. He realized that Jade's story had fogged his mind. He grimaced, then looked at his son and nodded. "Will you grate the cheese for me?"

Sean ran to the bar and climbed onto a stool, waiting as Declan set the cheese, grater, and bowl down before him. "How come you smoke cigarettes, dad? Jacob says that you're an idiot for doing it and that anybody who's that stupid shouldn't be telling stories on the news."

Declan tried to suppress his sigh, his patience wearing thin at just one more mention of the man's name. "It is a bad habit that I got into when I was studying for the bar exam. I was working, going to

182

school, studying, and trying not to go crazy, so I started because I needed help stay awake."

"But Dad, Jacob says you're going to die because you do it and then he's going to get stuck with me."

Stupid man, Declan thought, but tried to look as though he was on the verge of laughter. "Sean, people do get sick from smoking. I can't promise that I won't get sick, but I can promise you Jacob won't be affected by it." He turned to grin at his son. "Now, are you done with that cheese?"

"Almost," he said, his eyes fixed on the task before him. "I love you, Dad," he said earnestly.

Declan blinked, moisture filling his eyes. "I love you too, Sean," he said, the image of Lindy Grahame's livid face still playing through his mind.

After they had finished their meal and Declan cleaned up the mess left by the preparations, Sean settled down in front of the television to watch a movie. Declan enjoyed the sight of the anticipatory smile on the boy's face, his eyes fixed with excitement on the screen.

Declan sat down on the couch with his laptop and all the notes he had taken that day spread on the coffee table order of importance. He knew that something was wrong, that he had overlooked something or missed something entirely. After he'd looked through everything again, he just could not find the answer He stared at the words that Lindy had spoken to him, his baflement only growing.

He grimaced as the phone in his pocket began to ring. He wasn't in the mood to deal with more, yet he couldn't ignore it. There was too much at stake.

"Yeah?" he snapped, impatient at the disturbance of his work.

"Mr. Burke?" a quiet, female voice asked.

"Yeah."

A long pause came over the line, then a sniff. "I - need you to stop looking for me. If I wanted to be found, I would have let them know where I am. Stop looking for me," she said, her voice so weak it was more of a whisper.

His body froze. "Who is this?" he asked, already knowing, but he needed to find a way to keep her talking.

"This - is Jade Rosenberg. Stop looking for me."

"Jade, I've only been looking for you for about fourteen hours. I haven't found anything that would tell me where you went. I haven't talked to anyone who could tell me anything of use," he said, his voice calm and soothing, hearing small sounds in the background that he could not identify, along with her breaths that were short and ragged.

"I don't want to be found. Todd doesn't know where to find me, because I never let him see what I really was. He's never known how to find me." And the phone went dead.

Chapter 14

"Believe something and the Universe is on its way to being changed. Because you've changed, by believing. Once you've changed, other things start to follow."

Diane Duane

Thirteen Years Ago

"So where have you been?" Bruce asked as Jade walked in the door, her dark hair flying around her shoulders, her green eyes alight.

"Todd and I went to UNC. His sister's on the cross-country team, so we all went for a run," she said with a smile.

"You were running until two in the morning?"

Jade shrugged. "We went for some food and talked for a while." She folded her arms. "If you were that worried about me, you could've called, you know." She pulled her cell phone from her pocket and waved it at him.

Bruce huffed out a breath, though didn't comment. Instead, he walked over to her and put his arm around her shoulders to guide her back to the porch.

"Jade, you are sixteen years old. You have no right to be staying out until two. Why would you think that was alright?" Bruce asked, his voice much quieter than usual, his arm still holding her close to him.

"I didn't think about what time it was, Dad. I was just hanging out," She said, watching as the moonlight shone on him. "Tell me what's wrong, Dad. You've been trying not to tell me something for a while now." Her eyes pleaded, begging him to share his troubles.

Bruce ran his hand back through his hair. "Jade honey, it looks like - honey, Portia and I are getting divorced. She and Mase are moving out this weekend" His eyebrows drew together, his arm still banded around her like he meant to shield her from this blow.

Jade gaped at him and shook her head. "But they can't, Dad. There has to be another way. Can't you go to counseling or something? Maybe if we all went together, we could be a family," she

189

said with tears in her eyes.

"We're done, Jade. There is no more trying for us. We're just finished." Bruce sighed and pressed on. "We both know how close you and Mase are and how much it would hurt you both to be away, so we're working out a way to keep you two close. We've been thinking of doing visitation type visits, so Mase would come here, or you could go to Portia's once or twice a month. We're not trying to hurt you guys. We're just trying to stop hurting each other," he said, his words sounding rehearsed like he'd practiced his speech before giving it to her.

Jade's shoulders drooped, and she stared down at her hands. "Mase is my brother, the only family I have other than you," she said, trying to suppress her tears.

Bruce shifted in his chair, his mouth drawn into a straight line. "You've been a good sister to that boy, honey. I'm glad that Portia and I were together, just to give you that kind of thing."

A quiver filled her stomach, and an ache filled her chest at the thought. She knew there was nothing she could do, though her mind continued to look for solutions. She hated the idea of Mase moving out, though she was determined that he would feel no loss at all. She would make things okay for him, no matter what it cost her

As Jade walked into her bedroom a few minutes later, it surprised her to find Mase asleep in her bed. His arms were wrapped around a pillow with the tracks of dried tears on his cheeks.

In the last year, he had grown so much. His skinny frame filled out and his shoulders broadened, the lines on his face squared out to show the man he would grow into. No matter the physical changes, the wounded little boy remained, still in need of reassurance.

She sighed and knelt down next to him. "Mase?" she asked in a quiet voice.

His eyes opened immediately, still rather fogged by sleep, but very much awake. "Jade, mom says we're leaving, just me and her. She says that you and Bruce can't come. She says it's over," he told her in a dull tone that was more poignant than any tears could have been.

Jade nodded. "Dad just told me. He also told me they're going to let you and I hang out still, so you don't have to worry," she said with a pathetic attempt at a smile.

"But I don't want you to stop being my sister, Jade. I need you to be my sister, I need you to be there all the time." His eyes were glassy when he sat up, his arms wrapped protectively around his knees.

Jade shook her head. "Nothing can stop you from being my brother, Mase. You will always be my brother, the only one I ever wanted. I promise you, absolutely promise that any time you need me, I'll come running. You never have to be afraid, Mase, never."

He unclenched his arms and leaned forward to hug her. "Think I could come over and have dinner with you guys too, 'cause Mom's cooking sucks," he said with a shaky grin.

Jade pulled him back to look into his face. "I'd bet Dad would teach you how to cook when you come and spend some time with us."

"That would be cool," he said, his eyes turning to meet hers. "I - I love you, Jade. Thanks for being my sister."

"I love you too, and I love being your sister." She took his hand and pulled him to his feet. "Now, get to bed, would you?"

After Mase left her room, Jade groaned and stretched out on her bed to stare up at the ceiling. She had no desire for sleep. All she wanted - she did not know what she wanted. She had found it such a comfort to have Mase around, to talk to someone who so obviously loved her. He'd been a distraction from the darkness, but that was being taken away from her. She would be left alone with the things that she had feared.

She lay there for a while, her body growing more tense the longer she lay there. She grimaced and got out of bed. She needed air, so she pulled on her running shoes and walked from the house.

"Where do you think you're going?" Bruce's voice asked from behind her.

Jade turned. "I need a walk, maybe a run, I just need to move."

"It is no time for you to be out. You--"

"Dad, please. Every time I close my eyes, all I see is fire. I just want air," she said, moving her arms up to soothe the goosebumps that formed on her arms.

"Fire?" Bruce asked. "What do you mean, you see fire?"

Jade shook her head. "Dad, you know there's something wrong with me. Mom was right. I think I'm evil or something. Every time I feel some stong

emotion, things around me move and--"
she pressed her hand to the cross that
hung around her neck. "This gets hot.
Mom said I was the devil's daughter We
never talk about that. I think I'm the
reason Portia wasn't faithful to you. I
think I made her do it." Tears poured from
her eyes, her shoulders shaking with the
force of her emotions.

"Never say that out loud, Jade.
Never," he said, taking her shoulders and
shaking her hard. "Please tell me you've
told nobody this."

Her mouth fell open. "Told anyone
that I'm wicked? Why would I do that?"

"I need to know, Jade."

Her heart pounded and sweat broke
out on her forehead. "Uh, no. I haven't
told anybody, but people might've seen. It
just happens sometimes."

He crushed her to his chest, his
entire body shaking. "Listen to me, Jade.
You have to learn to control your
emotions. You can't ever let anyone see

those things."

"I don't try to, Dad. I--"

He pulled her back and shook her
again. "There is no try. There is only do.
You WILL learn to control your emotions."

She pulled free of him, flicking her
eyes around in search of an escape. "Tell
me what's going on, Dad. I have to know.
This is MY life. You can't keep these things
from me."

He slumped down onto a chair and
buried his face in his hands. "Jade, I
can't. I--"

"You have to tell me!" she shouted,
the porch around them vibrating like the
aftershock of an earthquake.

Bruce jumped to his feet, though he
was thrown back at a wave of force that
radiated from his daughter. He tried to
stand, but he couldn't move. All he could
do was stare at Jade.

The mix of fear, anxiety, and sorrow
compounded inside her until there was no
hope to control it at all. She smelled

smoke, then felt the burn as the necklace heated. The cross burned her.

Another sob escaped her, and she fell to her knees, clutching at the burned skin. The vibrations stopped. The world quieted. The only sounds were Jade's sobs of pain.

Bruce knelt down next to her and rested his hand on her back. "I'm sorry. I'm so sorry, Jade." He repeated those words over and over, tears sliding down his cheeks as well.

"What am I?" she whispered, nausea filling her belly.

"I don't know what we are, Jade. I really don't. All I know is that you have to keep it secret."

"Why?"

"Because they'll kill you if they find out what you can do."

Chapter 15

"The truth is rarely pure and never simple."

Oscar Wilde

The Present

"Hello?"

"Mase, who's Todd?" Declan asked in a rush as he pulled out of his sister's driveway.

The idea of the sleepover with his cousins had thrilled Sean, and thankfully, his sister had been understanding. It was a relief to have her support. He needed to be able to focus on Jade without having to worry about his son.

"Todd? I don't remember--" Mase paused, then let out a surprised sound. "Jade's first boyfriend. Todd was Jade's first boyfriend."

"Last name and where can I find him?"

"I don't have any idea, man. I know they keep in contact, but I haven't talked to the guy in several years."

199

Declan clenched his hands on the wheel so hard that his knuckles turned white. "It's important. Jade called me. She's alive, Mase. She called my cell phone and told me to stop looking for her She told me that nobody knows where she is, that Todd never knew where she was. She's trying to help us find her man," he said, his mind trying to take him back to any small detail, anything that could show him the way.

"She called you? She called YOU? Why would--"

"Shut up, Mase. I've spent less than a day doing my best to find information, which is scaring the people that have her They had her call to throw me off, but all they did is piss me of, so let's figure this thing out. Now, find out Todd's last name and call me back, faster than you've ever done anything in your life, kid." He ended the call and texted Frank to let him know what was going on.

Now he knew that finding Jade was

of the utmost importance, he would stop at nothing to save her "So you want me to look for Todd, your first boyfriend. What did you find out when you were a teenager, Jade? What did you find out that you told Todd?" He thought for a long moment, then nodded. "You and Todd have been friends for a long time. Most people have a hard time remaining friends with their exes, but not you. You have very few connections, so when you make one, you try to hold on, try to keep yourself from feeling utterly alone. Loneliness is all around you, because no one knows you, but you have your dad, you have Mase, and you have Todd to keep you from the utter lack of connections. That's your way." He rubbed his brow while he drove. "You figured something out in high school and you didn't want Bruce to know." His mind spun, trying to think what this could be.

He sighed and drummed his fingers on the wheel, opening the window as he lit a cigarette. He pulled the smoke into his lungs, hoping for clarity, for the jump in his system that so often gave him insight. He grimaced when nothing came to him other than the plea in Jade's voice when she'd called him.

He let out a groan of relief as his phone rang, answering it as quickly as he could. "Yeah," he barked into it.

"His name is Todd Logan. Bruce already called him. He's going to meet you at the same church you had me meet you at," Mase said in such a rush, it was difficult to understand what he'd said.

Declan grimaced. All he'd wanted was to talk to the man on the phone, though he supposed it would be better to meet him in person. He wasn't sure what to make of the whole situation, but he knew Jade needed him to hurry and figue things out.

Declan narrowed his eyes when he got out of his car, surprised to see a man already on the steps with a cigarette held between his first two fingers.

"You're Declan Burke?" the man asked and got to his feet.

"I am. And you are?" Declan asked, turning on the recording app while he lit himself another cigarette.

"I'm Lieutenant Todd Logan, National Guard," he said lamely, his eyes moving over the area in a nervous way.

Declan nodded. "Alright, Lieutenant Logan, I need to ask you a few questions about--"

"About Jade," he finished, sitting back down on the steps. He shook his head wearily. "Bruce told me. He said you're looking into finding her"

Declan sat next to the man, handing him the copy he'd made of the notes he had taken of his conversation with Jade.

Todd looked them over carefully, the muscle in his jaw going tight. "I don't understand. I haven't talked to her in a few months or more. We kind of had - a falling out. My wife doesn't like the fact that we're still friends, so we just sort of stopped talking. I don't know why she'd mention me."

"Were you dating?"

Todd shook his head. "We dated in high school, right about the time her life started going downhill. I tried to help her tried to do everything I could, but I was sixteen - and stupid." He ran his hand over his eyes. "We found out about her brother and - just thinking that maybe she'd finally have something normal in her life, I went with her to see him." He took a long drag on his cigarette. "Seriously messed up guy."

"You went to see him?" Declan asked, a tightness in his chest.

Todd nodded. "We did. He was eighteen or nineteen and lived in this dumpy trailer out in the woods--" He broke off, turning to shoot Declan a fevered stare. "That's it. He took her." He jumped to his feet and sent his cigarette flying as he began running down the steps toward his car.

Declan got there first, his hands raised in supplication as Todd took out his keys. "The cops are already there. We can't just go charging in there--"

"Yes, I can. I am the reason he even knew about her. I am responsible--"

"No, you're not. People are always looking for ways to blame themselves for things that have nothing to do with them. You took your teenage girlfriend to meet her brother when you were both teenagers. Tell me what happened."

Todd wrenched his arm free and got into his car. "Come if you want," he snapped.

Declan grimaced, but got into the passenger seat, his hands like ice while he struggled to swallow. "So tell me, Lieutenant, what is your wife going to think of this?"

"She's pissed," he said and began driving, his eyes fixed before him on the roads that would take him out of the city.

"Jade's just - I don't love her, but I can't just let her suffer. She's been through enough."

"Can you give me something more specific? How has she sufered?"

He sighed, his mouth tightening. "When she told me about her mom and I realized what it may mean to her, I freaked out a little, but I got over it. She'd never been open with anybody, about anything, but she told me about Lindy. She tried to break up with me because of it. She was terrified she'd turn out to have Huntington's too. She really tortured herself with it." He swallowed hard. "She convinced herself that she had to be crazy, that she imagined things that happened to her--"

"Like what?"

Todd shook his head. "Like a weekend that she went to visit Mase and came very close to being raped by Mase's older brother. Mase was barely twelve, and he beat the crap out of the guy, but Jade would never admit anything happened. She just convinced herself that she had dreamed it. Guys have always treated her like a mattress, but she talked herself into believing that she had deserved that kind of thing."

"Is that what you did?" Declan asked, no accusation in his voice.

Todd nodded slowly. "I did. She was hot, and I was nothing but hormones at that time. When I broke up with her, I thought she'd be mad, but she just told me she was sorry." He shook his head, shrugging as though to shrug of the weight of guilt. "Since she was never mad, we stayed friends and - and--"

"And you continued sleeping together," Declan finished and the picture he had formed of Jade changed. It was clear how lonely her life must have been, how much she had indeed put herself through.

Todd nodded. "She never really even understood what a friend was because she had Mase and she had me. Mase was her brother, no matter what, and I just used her."

"So she kept her distance from everyone, only allowing people to see the surface and very little of that."

"Exactly."

"So tell me about when you went to see Trenton," Declan said, the picture of Jade forming before him.

He saw the young girl who faced a boyfriend who was like so many at that age, her confidence at its lowest. She would have thought that finally she may have the family she had yearned for.

Todd's face went hard. "My sister was at UNC, told me she had seen this guy that looked so much like Jade that it was like seeing her, with shorter hair. The guy was working maintenance, so I checked him out. He'd been raised in a load of foster homes, at least ten, and was nothing but a loser. I walked up to the guy and told him I knew who he was and that he had a sister." He swallowed hard. "He stared at me, looking like I just hit him with a brick before, all he said was okay. That was it. We arranged for me and Jade to drive out to his place. I don't even know how I convinced him to do it. He didn't show any interest at all in meeting her, but somehow, he gave me directions." He grimaced. "I didn't tell Jade any of it, I just picked her up and started driving out there. I thought it was going to be the best surprise that anybody had ever given. I can still see the look on her face when he opened the door. She was about ready to faint." He tightened his grip on the steering wheel. "I introduced them, told them who they were, and stood back thinking I was the best thing ever." He tugged on his earlobe and swallowed hard. "He stared at her for a minute, then said, 'So you're the one they decided was good enough to keep? You don't look like much more than a whore.' She stood there and stared at him like she didn't hear a word.

He stepped down out of the trailer, then tossed his head back, and spit on her. All she did was stand there, then took a step back, wiped the loogie of her face, and rested her hand over the necklace she always wore."

Declan blinked. The necklace. There it was, but why? Why, when it was important enough to her as a teenager did she hide it behind her books as an adult? Why did it look as though she tried to get to it when she was fighting for her life?

"When did she get the necklace?" he asked, the back of his neck prickling.

"When she started losing contol of her power."

Declan turned his head to look at the man. "Power?" he asked, his skin suddenly cold.

Before Declan could even react, Todd jabbed a needle into his leg. It took only a moment for the world to go grayscale on him, but he fumbled, trying to reach his phone. It was already recording and would upload onto the cloud, though he didn't know how long it would be until anyone would think to check there. His hand went limp while an icy chill worked its way through him.

Chapter 16

"Whoever fights monsters should see to it that in the process he does not become a monster. And if you gaze long enough into an abyss, the abyss will gaze back into you."

Friedrich Nietzsche

One Week Ago

Portia swirled the wine in her glass and smiled at the man who watched her She enjoyed the way men's eyes followed her She always had.

Her last face lift had helped to smooth out the few lines on her skin, though she wasn't pleased with the results. The fact the man, who was at least ten years younger than her watched her in such a besotted way soothed her in a way that nothing else could. The adulation of men was her due, and she would not give it up without a fight.

The man stepped closer to her his blue eyes fixed on the swell of her enhanced breasts. "I don't mean to make this sound like a line, but don't I know you?" he asked with a smile.

She ran her eyes over his

well-tailored suit that he'd paired with a black t-shirt. It was a casual, classy look that she liked very much, though more, she liked the religious medal hung around his neck.

She wasn't a religious person herself. A man who was willing to wear a symbol of faith was usually one who had a lot of pent up passion. She always found it immensely rewarding to deal with them.

Portia ran a finger down her throat, a coquettish smile on her lips. "It does sound like a line, but the classics remain classics because of how well they work." She motioned to the empty chair next to her, eager to play with a man with such good taste and money to spare.

He pulled the chair out, his eyes fixed on her. "I really do think we've met, though," he said as he drummed his fingers on the table.

She took a sip of her wine. "Maybe we should get to know each other so we can figure this out," she purred.

"Maybe we should," he agreed and offered his hand. "I'm Marrok."

She rested her hand in his. "I'm Portia DaCosta," she said in a husky voice.

Marrok snapped his fingers. "Jade Rosenberg's mom," he said with a wide smile.

Portia had to fight to prevent the scowl she would normally wear at even the mention of that girl. "Jade is not my daughter. She was my step-daughter many years ago."

Marrok tipped his head to the side. "That's right. I'm sorry. I should have remembered that. My son had quite a thing for Jade at one point. I can't say I ever approved."

She took a far longer swallow of wine. "I can understand that. The little brat still has my son wrapped around her finger."

He narrowed his eyes. "There was something strange about her too, wasn't there?" he asked hesitantly.

Portia could no longer hold back her scowl. "Strange is hardly the word for it. The girl is a freak. I never believed in supernatural stories, but that girl made me believe."

He tapped his fingers on the table. "I have to admit, I did wonder There's something about her that either entices or repels, depending on the person."

Portia nodded. "Makes my skin crawl. She was a hellion as a teenager" A shudder of fear moved over her at even the memory of the years she'd been married to Bruce.

Marrok leaned forward and rested his hand over hers. "Portia, there are many things out there that most people don't know about. My family and I take care of those things." He waved a hand and a man and woman walked over from another table. "If you tell us more, we can save people from her depravity. It's our job, Portia."

She looked at the three, seeing the resemblance between them, though also the intensity. These were zealots, ones who lived by the sword and believed themselves to be heroes. If there were people out there who took out creatures like Jade, she was all for it.

"What do you want to know?"

"What can she do?" the woman asked.

Portia took another swallow of wine before she spoke. "Things move when she's angry. Sometimes, it's almost like an earthquake." She recalled how things would fall to the ground when Jade was in trouble, though more, she remembered the feeling in the air

It was as if the air stopped working. She would gasp for breath and feel no relief. That girl had tried to kill her She knew it was true. She would not let that stand for even one more moment.

"Telekinesis," the woman said and leaned forward. "What kinds of things weaken her? It would be subtle. Creatures like her don't show their weaknesses easily, but since you lived in the same house, you might have noticed something."

Portia pursed her lips. "She's got an allergy to salt. We once mixed up our bowls of cantaloupe. I had salted mine. She was in the hospital for a week."

The three eyed each other. "Demon?" the younger man asked in a quiet voice.

"Maybe," the woman responded, turning to face Portia again. "We could use your help. Jade is a danger and we are here to protect the world from monsters like her. Will you help us?" she asked, the fervor in her eyes a compelling sight.

Portia didn't hesitate for even a moment. "What can I do?" she asked in a steady voice.

Chapter 17

"We forge the chains we wear in life."

Charles Dickens

The Present

Declan blinked, then blinked again. His head swam and his mouth was as dry as paper. On top of all that, he couldn't move.

He looked around, and his heart sank. He sat in the center of what looked like a shed, bound by his hands and feet to a chair. In the corner, Jade Rosenberg was bound in the same way.

His heart rate spiked when he got a good look at her. Jade's face was a mass of bruises. Some were the fading yellow-green color of old bruises, while others were red and swollen, indicating she'd been hurt recently. He guessed that must have been done to her when she gave him the message about Todd.

"Jade?" he croaked, his tongue hardly able to form the word.

She didn't look up.

He fought to loosen his arms,

though all he managed was to cause himself pain. The restraints were heavy and were the color of rust, though their texture was smooth. Could they be iron? They looked similar to something he'd seen in a medieval movie, although he couldn't say he'd examined the shackles in those movies closely enough to say for sure.

He shifted around to see if he might be able to hop toward her, but the chair didn't move even the tiniest bit. What kind of freaks had iron manacles and chairs that were bolted to the floor?

Looking around the shed made it clear they were likely serial killers. The hooks in the ceiling and dark stains under those hooks made that obvious.

"What were you thinking?" a voice he hadn't heard before said from the other side of the shed door

"I was trying to clean up your mess. Why did you keep her alive?" Todd asked in a loud enough voice to make it clear they were in a place where no one could overhear them.

"She's alive because she's pregnant. Heather thinks we should keep it alive and train it to use against the others."

Declan's heart beat so hard in his chest, it hurt. Heather The woman who had seduced Ronnie to keep him away from Jade on the night she was kidnapped. That woman wanted to raise Jade's baby? What was going on?

"Heather is a moron. If you keep it alive, it'll turn on you. There is no way that's a good idea," Todd said in a weary way, as though being the voice of reason was an exhausting pursuit.

"You walked out on us, son. You chose a different path. Coming back here with some reporter who will most certainly be missed and criticising the way we do things is not the way this family gets things done."

Declan cursed himself for a fool. The moment Jade called him, he should have done all the research he could rather than rushing out like a rookie on his first case. He knew better, but he'd done it, anyway.

Since there was nothing he could do about his mistake, he gathered as much information as possible while he looked for a way out. The information those two were spilling out could give him a clue of what was going on. Hopefully, there would be a piece that would help to get them out.

Todd continued on. "Coming back and seeing what you guys are doing makes me glad I left. What were you thinking leaving that note? If she'd just disappeared, it would've been easy to--"

"What note?"

"The ransom note you left at Jade's place."

There was a pause. "I left no ransom note."

Declan listened harder, trying to understand what they said. If it was true that they hadn't written the ransom note, then who had and why? The story began to shift around in his mind until a shadowy picture formed, one that both made sense and gave him more questions.

The voices grew further away until nothing more could be heard. He didn't understand what was going on. He wished he'd worked with his film crew or even talked to Frank before he left.

He stilled, wondering if it was possible that his phone might still be recording. If Todd hadn't bothered to search him, it might still be in his pocket. His producer would look at the document all his recordings would have made, yet that wouldn't be until the next day, unless he was at the station later than usual.

He looked at his jeans, trying to see if his phone was there. He'd stopped carrying a wallet years before, his money and ID kept in a money clip in his font pocket. He could feel it there, along with his keys. He wasn't sure if he could feel his phone on the other side or not.

"I think Trenton did it," a whispery

voice said.

Declan looked over at Jade again, able to see that her eyes were open and fixed on him. "That seems like an odd thing to do," he said in hopes to keep her talking.

Jade moved her head in what could have passed for a nod. "He's messed up," she breathed.

"I didn't get to talk to him yet."

"Lucky you," Jade said, her lips quivering a tiny bit.

Declan smiled in return, glad to see that there was life left inside her "Can you tell me about him? Todd said you met him when you were a teenager," he prodded, able to see that she needed to talk.

Jade's lips curled in a sneer "I met Trenton when I was sixteen. We didn't get along, but after a few years, he contacted me again. He apologized for the way he treated me and we started talking." She shifted around in her chair, her movements slow and weak. "He spent his life in foster care and juvy on drug charges. He turned into a hard man, but not a bad one. He just needed the compassion that no one ever gave him. I needed the same thing, so for a few years, we were family."

There was a heaviness in Declan's stomach. The picture of Jade he'd formed in his mind changed again. She wasn't the victim, the mattress Todd had made her out to be. She was a compassionate woman who'd learned early in life that chosen family was often more loyal than the biological variety.

Jade swallowed hard. "Trenton was the one who told me that Lindy wasn't in the nursing home my dad had always told me she was in. He convinced me to talk to her. He told me that having a disease which was eating away at her mind and body was the only reason she'd done what she did to me." She closed her eyes and shook her head. "That may be true, but her hatred of me is real. It hasn't changed

- and she's right to hate me."

"What do you mean, Jade?"

She opened her eyes and looked straight at him. "Do you believe in magic?" she asked, her body stif as she gazed at him.

Declan blinked. It was such an odd question, though something about it probed at his memory. He had never truly thought about it before.

He'd read a few fantasy books, along with a few fantasy and horror mashups, but he'd never guessed some of it might be true. He believed in God, so the idea that there was more to the world than he could see probably shouldn't have surprised him at all.

As the thought of *magic* passed through his mind, a few puzzle pieces clicked into place. Lindy had tried to kill her daughter because she believed the girl was evil. If a woman in her condition saw something she couldn't explain, calling it evil would make sense to her Was it possible that Jade had some kind of extrasensory perception or a power of some sort?

"I - I've never given it much thought," he said in a cautious tone.

When those words left his mouth, the last clue settled into place. The necklace. It was tarnished like it hadn't been polished in a long time - or like it was iron. The manacles around his wrists were also iron. He'd read enough to recall how both salt and iron were used to ward off supernatural beings.

His mouth worked silently for a few seconds. Nature surrounded the house where Jade had grown up. She'd hidden an iron cross on her bookshelf at her home, which was also very close to nature. Every picture in her office other than the one of the fire was of nature.

"A fairy," he gasped, his eyes wide as saucers.

Jade swallowed hard and gave a slow nod. "I'm unnatural. Wicked. I deserve--"

"No." He shook his head. "You're not unnatural or wicked, Jade. I was a cop for ten years before I became a reporter and an attorney before that. I've seen both the best and the worst that humanity has to offer, and there is no race or class or condition that makes a person inherently bad. It's a choice. Circumstances and genetics change the likelihood of a person making bad decisions, but none of it makes a person *wicked.*" His scathing tone put air quotes around the word.

Jade sat still for a moment, then she turned her eyes down. "I've spent my life trying to understand what I was and why things happened. Now, I don't care. All I want is to make sure my baby gets out of here and isn't used by these people."

Declan looked around, searching for any way out. "Okay, I have to ask. Why did you tell me Todd never knew where you were?" he asked, moving his hands around in the cuffs to see if there was any

229

way to loosen them.

"I couldn't just say look at the police commissioner's family, they're the ones who have me. I hoped it was vague enough that they'd think I was just out of it."

Declan would have face palmed himself if he could have moved his hands. Logan. How had he not put that together? Frank had been told by the commissioner to drop the case. It had made him wonder He should have looked into that right away. It was on his list of things to look into. Thankfully, since it was in his notes, his producer could look into it himself or hand it over to someone else. That was some small comfort at least.

He hated the idea of Frank being forced to investigate his disappearance. He might be crotchety, but they'd been friends since the first case they'd worked together. Frank would not take it well, especially if he figured out the actual truth.

Declan grimaced. He needed to stop

imagining what might happen in the future and start making a plan to get them out of there. He would not allow those people to take Jade's baby, nor would he allow them to kill either of them. He just had to figure out how to stop them.

He jerked when the door opened, furious with himself for taking so long. He didn't have any idea how to get them out.

Chapter 18

"Fire wants to burn

Water wants to flow

Air wants to rise

Earth wants to bind

Chaos wants to devour

..."

Cassandra Clare

The Present

Declan clenched his hands into fists to keep them from shaking. Three men and a woman stepped into the shed, all four of them bearing a striking resemblance to each other. The woman was attractive, her blue eyes both striking and direct, though they were cold as glaciers.

Todd stood further back, his hands shoved into his pockets while he glared at Declan. The man in the group's front looked like he must be the father of the three. He was an older version of Todd, with a few lines around his mouth and the same blue eyes as the woman.

The last guy looked rough. He clearly hadn't showered in several days and had a chemical odor mixed with his unwashed scent. Then there were the pinpoint pupils which told the truth of his issue.

Since all four of them stood in font of him, Declan understood they had no intention of allowing him to live. Images passed through his mind of his son looking out the window, waiting for him to come home. He could hear the questions Sean would ask. He wondered if April would come back when she found out they had killed him.

More pictures passed through his mind, though they weren't of his son. Instead, they were of all the people he'd talked to in the last day. Mase. Ronnie. Frank. Bruce. Lindy. Juan. But it was Juan who really stuck out in his mind.

Declan had an odd feeling when he left Jade's office. He felt like he'd missed something or that there had been a clue mixed in with Juan's answers. He needed to figure out what it could have been.

"Who knows that you were meeting with Todd?" the older man asked abruptly.

"How did you get my cell number?"

he asked in return.

Despite the fact he knew it was coming, that didn't make the blow any easier to take. Declan's ears rang and his jaw throbbed while the man shook out his hand. Any hope he'd held onto that they would let him go faded away when Todd stepped forward.

Declan had a feeling that things were about to get very serious for him. He hoped he'd be able to hold out, but he'd interviewed a soldier who was held by the Talaban. He knew everyone had a breaking point.

Todd didn't strike him, though. Instead, he walked over to where Jade sat and took a handful of her hair "How many people knew we were meeting?"

Jade met Declan's eyes and he could see something there. There was an odd mix of resignation and rage in her eyes. He could see that she had reached the end of her endurance.

Whatever her plan was, he needed

to help her however he could. It would be far easier if his hands were free, so that was his first goal.

"Depends if you took my phone. If you did, then just a few people. If you didn't, then my producer, the cops, my old partner, my dad, and a few thousand others," he said with a mocking smile.

The guy who was high jumped forward and started trying to dig into his pockets. When he couldn't, he tugged on Declan's arms to get him closer to a standing position. Declan didn't move.

The guy fumbled around in his own pockets for keys, muttering profanities while he worked.

"Joss, knock it off," the man snapped, but Joss didn't.

He worked harder, fitting the key into the lock and turning it before Heather or the other man could stop him.

Declan shifted to free himself until the barrel of a gun was jammed into the side of his head. "Move and die," the man barked.

He froze, his eyes fixed on the man's. "What's this about? How can you justify any of this to yourselves? Jade is innocent."

He scoffed. "Innocent? Things like her have been entrancing men with no repercussions since the beginning of time, and you tell me it's innocent?"

"Entrancing men? What do you think Heather did to Ronnie? Ae you planning to shackle her to a chair as well?"

"Heather has been disciplined for her whoring." He sneeed over his shoulder at Heather befoe he jabbed a finger at Jade. "That thing has aleady tried to seduce my son even after it was disciplined."

"Disciplined?" Declan asked through his teeth, hoping to distract Joss from his search for the phone.

"Disciplined," he epeated. "Thee's only one way to deal with corrupt women."

"And what about deviant men who like to grope women that are bound to a chair?" Jade asked, her voice far stonger than it had yet been.

"Shut your mouth, slut," Joss shouted and stepped between the man, the gun, and Declan.

Before the man could remedy his mistake, Declan moved. He was all too aware of how the gun changed things. The fact he was unarmed had not left his mind.

All the information he'd gathered told him that Jade was their best hope of escape. Iron bands shackled her, but there was an iron cross in her home, and that iron sculpture on her desk. She must have built up an immunity to it over the years. He didn't know how much help she would need to get free, but he would do whatever it took to save them both.

He hooked his arm around Joss' neck and yanked him over, shielding himself from the gun. He had little faith that a man who would beat his daughter for having sex would work to save his son when he'd been responsible for Declan being freed. He needed to find a better shield or a weapon of his own.

The door opened, slamming so hard into the wall that it cracked. Declan looked in that direction, though no one was there. He knew it must be Jade, so he had to draw the man's attention away from her.

"Everybody knows where I am. The commissioner can't sweep your crimes under the rug anymore," he taunted, his arm tight around Joss' neck.

The man whirled toward the door with the gun pointed in that direction. Declan tossed Joss to the side and stepped forward, grabbing the man's wrist and turning him as he went. With a quick move of his hip and arm, he disarmed the man and had him on the ground with the gun pointed at the back of his head.

"Burke, you shoot him, I kill her."

Todd yelled, still holding Jade by the hair

Declan moved so his back was to the wall, his eyes taking in everything around him. Because Todd was the greatest threat at the moment, he kept the gun pointed at him while he watched the others closely. He did not feel more secure with the gun in his hand. If anything, he felt less safe.

When he'd been a cop, there had only been a few times that he'd needed to draw his gun. Of those times, he always had backup, a partner he knew and trusted. Right then, he trusted Jade, but he wasn't sure how they could both get out of that situation.

Todd tightened his grip on Jade's hair, his eyes fixed on Declan. "You know you can't win this. Put the gun down and we'll let you walk out of here," he said in a calm voice.

Jade scoffed. "Do you really think he's that stupid, Todd?" she asked, her eyes fixed on Declan. "Mark Logan, his sons Todd and Joss, and his daughter Heather have been hunting and killing people for years. They convinced Portia DaCosta to help them capture me."

Declan blinked, his mouth going dry when he realized what she was doing. If his phone was in his pocket, which he was sure it was, she had just left a record that his producer could take to the police. The woman was a genius.

Todd gritted his teeth. "Get it," he said, as though it was an order to a guard dog.

Heather grabbed for Declan's wrist, pivoting him forward and around before she flipped him over her shoulder He landed hard and felt a snap in his arm before a bolt of red hot pain radiated from that point. A moan of pain escaped him when Heather's foot nudged his broken arm and the world went gray around him.

He blinked, then blinked again, surprised that he could make that move at all. He expected to be dead.

What he found instead was that
everything around him was still and quiet.
Not one sound. Not one movement. The
world was quiet as the grave.

"Are you okay?"

He turned his head blearily, seeing
a pair of green eyes barely visible through
swollen bruises all around them. He tried
to sit up, but he was too lightheaded to
manage it. "I have been better You?" he
asked in an offhand tone.

Her lips curved. "Best week of my
life," she said with a sigh. "I can't hold
them for long. Any chance you can get up
and unlock these things for me? I've been
trying all week, but I don't know the inner
workings of the lock, so I wasn't able to
move anything inside it."

He blinked again and again, then
let out a chuckle. "Least I can do since you
just saved my life," he said and shifted
around to get to his feet.

He did his best to move in a way
that wouldn't jostle his arm, though the

pain continued on. He didn't look, not wanting to distract himself from the simple task of standing. No matter how easy it should have been, it was excruciatingly difficult.

"Talk to me, would you? Tell me how you're holding them?" he panted, closing his eyes for a few seconds when he got to his knees.

"When I'm around nature, I can move things with my mind," she said in such a blase tone, it was like she'd just told him she was a publicist.

He opened his eyes and looked at her, waiting for her to say more.

Jade let out a slow sigh. "When I was a teenager, it was really difficult for me to control that ability. Any emotional spike and things around me would move. My dad gave me this cross that had an iron plate on the back. After I started wearing it, when that ability would rise up, the iron would burn me and that would bring me back to reality. After a while, it stopped working, but by that time, I'd learned to guard my emotions."

Declan walked to where Joss stood and picked up the keys that had fallen to the ground at his feet. "I saw the necklace at your condo, as well as the sculpture in your office."

She swallowed hard. "It's a reminder to be careful more than anything else," she mumbled, her eyes turned down.

"How did these idiots find out about you?" he asked before the light dawned. "The fight Mase was supposed to throw. You did something, didn't you? You stopped them from coming after him."

Jade blew out a long breath. "I only planned to tell them to leave him alone, but one of them told me he was going to kill Mase and I kind of lost it. I pinned him to the ceiling and told him he needed to rethink that idea."

Declan chuckled, fumbling slightly as he fit the key into the lock. "If my sister

244

had that kind of power, my ex-wife might've lost an eye."

Her lips quirked again. "I cannot understand people. I've known since I was a kid that Portia hated me. But the idea that she would work with these people is just painful. Mase is family to me. I cannot understand how she made a guy like him."

Declan sighed in relief when he got the key to turn, though his sigh changed to a gasp when he saw the state of Jade's wrists. They were red and raw. The skin swollen and clearly painful. They looked more like she'd been held for months rather than the week it had been.

She moved her arms slowly, rubbing at her shoulders while she made slight movements of the rest of her body. He wasn't sure how long it would take her to be able to move freely again, though it was clear it would take some time.

A sound behind him made him whirl around. Heather was in the same place, though she had moved a small bit.

It looked like they needed to get out of there as fast as possible.

"I'm losing it," Jade breathed, her eyes closed while a look of deep concentration passed over her face.

He held his arm as close to his body as he could and ofered his hand to Jade. "Come on. Let's--"

"Wicked!" a voice shrieked from the doorway.

Declan turned, his mouth agape when he saw Lindy Grahame standing there. Her body tremored far more than it had when he first met her, and her eyes were wild with a mix of madness and what looked like fear. She stood there with a man he could only assume was Trenton, the resemblance between Jade and the man rather startling.

When he looked more closely at Trenton, he finally understood. Everywhere he'd gone that day, he'd seen that man. He was at the diner, at the police station, at Jade's ofice, and at the

246

coffee shop where he'd had lunch. He had been following Declan all day, and Declan hadn't even noticed.

He felt like a fool, though the slavish way he stood with his mother made Declan worry. There was something very wrong with both of them. He could see the jerkiness to the way Trenton moved, and a bit of drool spilled from the side of his mouth.

He'd done some research on Huntington's after Mase brought it up. It was clear that Trenton had it. The muscle spasms along with dificulty swallowing, were among the symptoms listed.

Lindy pointed a shaky finger at Jade and cursed. "Satan's child. That's why you can do these unnatural things. You're the devil's girl!"

Jade's eyes were blank, her face expressionless. She didn't speak. She stood and stared at the ground in front of her. The abused child.

Declan raised his good hand and

stepped in front of Jade. "We need to get out of here. These--"

"You!" Lindy bawled, her accusing finger now pointed at him. "How dare you speak to me. You're one of them!" Her voice was slurred in a manner that would have made him think she was drunk under normal circumstances.

If it was a medication which had kept her symptoms away, it was likely she hadn't taken them. That mood swing was more violent than he'd seen in the few videos he'd watched in his research.

He kept his eyes fixed on Trenton. The man stood shakily, his eyes fixed on Jade. Green eyes. Just like Bruce. Bruce Rosenberg, who'd given his daughter an iron cross to wear. It came from him. Bruce was a fairy.

He knew nothing about the genetic implications, but at a guess, he thought it was likely Trenton had the same ability Jade had. He wasn't sure if Trenton had hidden that from Lindy or if she knew and chose to ignore it.

He took a step forward, stopping when he smelled the smoke.*Dear God, she set the shed on fire!*

Declan looked back at Jade. "You do know she's crazy, right? Huntington's might have given her mood swings, but this is way beyond the norm. Maybe the medication they gave her did it. I don't know. What I do know is that you are not wicked. You're Bruce Rosenberg's daughter. And you're Mase's sister. Nothing else matters right now. Mase needs you."

Jade blinked, then blinked again. Slowly, she met his eyes. "Let's get out of here," she said, and a feeling of power filled the air.

Declan's eyes went wide when she stepped forward, wrapped her hand around his good one, and suddenly, they weren't in the shed anymore. His head swam and his ears popped, although nothing had ever felt so good to him. They were out of that burning shed.

It took a moment for his eyes to take in everything around them. They stood in the middle of the woods with a picturesque log cabin with the burning shed not far from it. The burning shed that the Logans remained inside of.

Jade stepped around him, her gait slow and pained, but she looked ready for anything. She gazed at that fire. Her hands were steady. She was willing to go back into that burning building to save people who had kidnapped her

Declan reached out and took her arm. "Jade, we--"

"We can't leave them," she stated with such conviction, he couldn't argue.

He tucked his broken arm tighter to his body and nodded. "Thanks for getting me out of there, Jade," he said while they rushed back toward the inferno.

She glanced over at him. "Thanks for trying to find me," she said in a defeated tone.

His stomach clenched when he heard the screams. It wasn't just screams of pain. It was also the mad rantings of an unbalanced woman.

"Wickedness!" she screeched over and over like some creature from a nightmare.

As they got closer, he could see Lindy's hands balled into fists while she pummeled Trenton. When he saw the figures in the burning shed who didn't move at all while flames engulfed their bodies, he understood. Lindy had just found out that her precious son had the same power Jade possessed.

Lindy let out a howl of rage and shoved Trenton from behind. He stumbled and fell into the flames, though he didn't fight to free himself. He stood and allowed the blaze to take him.

Chapter 19

"All truths are easy to understand once
they are discovered; the point is to
discover them."

Galileo Galilei

The Present

Flashing lights. The clamour of voices. The smell of smoke. That quiet, secluded forest was now an epicenter of activity.

Declan declined when the third paramedic tried to get him to lie on a gurney. They'd given him a sling to immobilize his arm and a painkiller, so he didn't think it was necessary to be rushed off to the hospital just yet. There was too much going on around him. He had to see how it would end.

Jade stepped away from a cop who'd been talking to her for the last twenty minutes and met Declan's eyes. Her lip wobbled before tears spilled down her cheeks. She'd been through hell and it showed all over her face.

Her body trembled with the horror of it all, but Declan could see a defiance in her as well. Her mother had not broken her. She may be damaged and very much in need of help, but she would heal.

He glanced at the police car that was just driving Lindy Grahame away and a heaviness filled his chest and limbs. It was a strange and terrible thing to see someone who was so disturbed that burning her own children alive had seemed like a good option to her He did not believe it was only the Huntington's that skewed her mind. He hoped that this time, they would keep her locked up.

"So looks like there's going to be an investigation into the department because of Commissioner Logan," Frank said, his arms folded while he scowled at the firefighters.

Declan nodded. "It's going to be a lot of hassle," he said agreeably.

Frank turned his scowl on Declan. "You were right, okay? I never should have stopped looking into this case, no matter what orders I got. It was stupid and irresponsible of me. If I had kept looking, I would have found Trenton and he would have been able to lead me here. This is on my head," he growled.

"Partially, but mostly, it's on the head of the people who kidnapped Jade."

Frank huffed. "There's things inside the house that indicates the Logans might have killed more than twenty people. There's an FBI task force on the way to look at everything."

Declan's heart sank. So many lives taken and there was no way to know if they were all innocent like Jade or if they might have truly been a danger There had to be a way to - his mind froze as the idea came to him.

He stepped away from Frank, hurrying to where Jade was being looked after by another paramedic. "Could you give us a minute?" he asked the woman, hardly looking at her as she stepped away.

Jade turned her battered face up to look at him. "You're thinking what I'm thinking, aren't you?" she asked in a dull tone.

Declan raised his brows. "If you're thinking that we should tell the world that there are people with power out there so we can hopefully prevent things like this from ever happening again, then yeah. I'm thinking what you're thinking."

Jade swallowed hard. "They won't believe us. They'll call us crazy."

"At first they will. Then others will come forward. You and your dad aren't the only ones."

She blinked, then let out a shaky breath. "I should have figured you'd guess the truth."

He tipped his chin down. "Once people accept that the world is bigger than we know. People who already know will come forward and corroborate what we're saying. We could change the world by telling your story."

Jade moved her arms, then relaxed them again. "I'd like to bring my child into a world that already knows what we are. I'd like my baby to know that it's okay to be different. I've been alone for so long, though. I'm not sure I know how to make that kind of adjustment."

Declan smiled. "Change is coming, Jade. I'm planning on being your first true friend, if you'll let me," he held out his left hand between them.

Jade smiled in return and carefully laid one of her damaged hands in his. "I'd like that," she said before her shoulders straightened. "Let's change the world, Declan."

My Facebook:

https://www.facebook.com/Shannon-Reber-1450668291923946/

My Twitter:

https://twitter.com/ShannonArtWrite

My Goodreads:

https://www.goodreads.com/author/show/14219796.Shannon_Reber

My Instagram

https://www.instagram.com/authorshannonreber/?hl=en

Other books by Shannon Reber

http://www.amazon.com/author/shannonreber

And The Shadows

Amplify (The Broken Truce Book 1)

The Silver Dime (A Short Story)

In The Works (The Light Bearer Prequel)
In Their Midst (The Light Bearer Book 1)
In Memory Of (The Light Bearer Book 2)

The Key (reprogramming the gods Book 1)

Ill-Fated (The Cintamani Chronicles Book 1)
Ill-Omened (The Cintamani Chronicles Book 2)
Ill-Starred (The Cintamani Chronicles Book 3)
The Cintamani Chronicles (The Complete Trilogy)

The Girl In White (A Madison Meyer Mystery Volume 1)
The Exiler (A Madison Meyer Side Story)
The Black Merchant (A Madison Meyer Mystery Volume 2)
The Dark Spirit (A Madison Meyer Side Story)
The Infernal Goddesses (A Madison Meyer Side Story)
The Thirteen Bends (A Madison Meyer

Mystery Volume 3)
The Mistaken Son (A Madison Meyer Side
Story)
The Team's Tales (The Madison Meyer Side
Stories)
The Shadow Walkers (A Madison Meyer
Mystery Volume 4)
The Trail of Ruins (A Madison Meyer
Mystery Volume 5)
The Fire of Hestia (A Madison Meyer
Mystery Volume 6)
The Second Chance (A Madison Meyer
Mystery Volume 7)
The Father's Scent (A Madison Meyer Side
Story)
The Writing on the Wall (A Madison Meyer
Mystery Volume 8)
The Summoning Charge (A Madison Meyer
Mystery Volume 9)
The Helping Hands (A Madison Meyer Side
Story)

Friends and Foes (The Druid Heirs book 1)
Life and Loss (The Druid Heirs book 2)
Peace and Peril (The Druid Heirs book 3)
The Druid Heirs (The Complete Trilogy)

Misery (A Short Story)

Cadger (The Annwyn Revolution Book 1)

Illusion

Gray (Awakening Book 1)
White (Awakening Book 2)

Black (Awakening Book 3)

The Stockades (The Uniters Code Book 1)
The Sepulcher (The Uniters Code Book 2)
The Stronghold (The Uniters Code Book 3)
The Sanctum (The Uniters Code Book 4)
The Shrine (The Uniters Code Book 5)
The Uniters Code (The Complete Series)

The Seer (The Seal of Solomon prequel)
The Puppeteer (The Seal of Solomon Book 1)
The Gatekeeper (The Seal of Solomon Book 2)
The Fire Wielder (The Seal of Solomon Book 3)
The Seal of Solomon (The Complete Series)

ABOUT THE AUTHOR

Shannon Reber was born a long time ago in a galaxy far, far away . . . or her imagination was anyway. She lives in western New York with her husband and a wide variety of both real and imaginary friends who often battle it out for dominance in her head. Who needs another normal person in this messed up world? Read her books, or the evil overlord will take control of her mind!

Made in the USA
Middletown, DE
20 August 2023

36614883R00156